c romance from

Lynne Graham

The all new Lynne Graham
large print collection gives you your
favourite glamorous Lynne Graham stories
in easier-to-read print.

Lynne Graham was born in Northern Ireland and has been a keen Mills & Boon® reader since her teens. She is very happily married, with an understanding husband who has learned to cook since she started to write! Her five children keep her on her toes. She has a very large dog, which knocks everything over, a very small terrier, which barks a lot, and two cats. When time allows, Lynne is a keen gardener.

EXPECTANT BRIDE

BY

LYNNE GRAHAM

MILLS & BOON

First published in Great Britain 1999
by Mills & Boon, an imprint of Harlequin (UK) Limited.
Large Print edition 2013
Harlequin (UK) Limited, Eton House,
18-24 Paradise Road, Richmond, Surrey TW9 1SR

© Lynne Graham 1999

ISBN: 978 0 263 23738 2

11834350

Harlequin (UK) policy is to use papers that are natural, renewable and recyclable products and made from wood grown in sustainable forests. The logging and manufacturing process conform to the legal environmental regulations of the country of origin.

Printed and bound in Great Britain
by CPI Antony Rowe, Chippenham, Wiltshire

CHAPTER ONE

'WHAT on earth are you wearing on your head?' Meg Bucknall demanded as she pressed the button for the service lift.

Ellie raised a self-conscious hand to the floral scarf which covered her hair. 'It'll keep the dust off.'

'Since when have you been so fussy?'

Ellie heaved a sigh and decided to be honest with the older woman. 'There's this guy who often works late on my floor…and, *well*, he's—'

'Making a nuisance of himself, is he?' Meg's round face tightened with disapproval but she wasn't surprised by the news. Even in an overall Ellie would attract keen male attention. Fashioned on petite but shapely lines, the young woman had hair so naturally fair it gleamed like silver, and clear green eyes enhanced by unexpectedly dark brows and lashes. 'I bet he thinks he's onto a sure thing with a humble cleaner. Old or young?'

'Young.' Ellie stood back to let Meg enter the lift

first. 'He's really getting on my nerves. I've been thinking about mentioning him to the supervisor.'

Meg grimaced. 'No, whatever you do, don't make it official, Ellie. If this lech works late, he must be quite important. Let's face it, you're more expendable than some business whizzkid!'

'Don't I know it.' Ellie sighed. 'It's still a man's world.'

'He must be pretty persistent if he's getting *you* down…' Meg frowned, thinking of how feisty Ellie could be, although nobody would ever think it to look at her. 'Look, you do my floor tonight and I'll do yours. That'll give you a break. Then maybe one of the other cleaners will consider doing a permanent switch with you.'

'But I haven't got security clearance to clean the top floor,' Ellie reminded the older woman reluctantly.

'Oh, never mind that!' Meg dismissed impatiently. 'Why should anyone need special permission just to polish floors and empty bins? But if the security guard does a round while you're up there, take yourself off out of sight if you can. Some of those blokes *would* report us. And don't go through those big double doors at the front.

That's Mr Alexiakis's office suite and I'm not allowed in there…OK?'

As the older woman pushed her trolley out onto the floor that was usually Ellie's responsibility, Ellie gave her a grateful smile. 'I really appreciate this, Meg.'

Ellie had never been on the top floor of the Alexiakis International building before. When she emerged from the service lift, she realised that the layout was different from the floors below. Rounding a corner, she saw a large, luxurious reception area to her right. Beyond it, all the lights had been turned off, but she could dimly see an impressive set of double doors in the gloom.

But when she looked to her left, another set of plainer double doors also greeted her at the far end of the corridor. She raised her eyebrows, but assumed the unlit passage closer to Reception housed the office suite that was off-limits. Deciding to start at the opposite end and work her way back along the corridor, Ellie relaxed. She was delighted by the prospect of any evening shift uninterrupted by Ricky Bolton and his suggestive remarks.

Her canvas-shod feet making little sound, Ellie opened one of the heavy double doors and had crossed the room to reach for the overflowing wastepaper basket before she registered that the interconnecting office beyond was still occupied. The door stood slightly ajar, spilling out the unmistakable sound of male voices.

Usually she would have announced her presence, but, having taken Meg's advice on board, she decided it would be wiser just to beat a quick, quiet retreat. The very last thing she wanted to do was get the older woman into trouble. Just as she was about to step back out again she heard male footsteps coming down the corridor, and practically had a heart attack on the spot.

Without even thinking about what she was doing, she shot behind the door to conceal herself, her heart hammering like a piston. The steps got closer and closer, and then stopped *right* on the other side of the open door. At that point Ellie just stopped breathing altogether.

In the rushing silence she could now hear every word of the dialogue carrying through from the office next door.

'...so as long as I continue to *appear* to be interested in acquiring Danson Components, Palco Technic will remain a sitting duck,' a dark-accented male drawl was murmuring with satisfaction. 'I'll make my move the minute the market opens on Wednesday.'

Ellie heard whoever else was on the other side of the door catch their breath audibly. She felt like a total idiot. What the heck had she been thinking of? The maintenance trolley parked outside supplied visible proof of her presence somewhere nearby.

However, the man in the doorway advanced no deeper into the room. To her surprise and relief, she heard him start back down the corridor much more quietly than he had walked up it. Ellie slowly sucked in much-needed air. She was creeping out from concealment on literal tiptoe when the door of the interconnecting office suddenly shot wide to frame an intimidating male, who seemed at that moment to be as tall as a skyscraper. She froze, green eyes huge in her flushed and discomfited face.

Eyes as black as pitch raked over her in a challenging appraisal as aggressive as a loaded gun.

'What the hell are you doing in here?' he shot at her in angry disbelief.

'I was just leaving—'

'You were hiding behind the door *listening*!' he contradicted in pure outrage.

'No, I wasn't listening.' Ellie was genuinely shocked by the level of his annoyance, and then, as she recognised him, her own tension rocketed right off the scale.

No, they hadn't met before, but there was a dirty great enormous portrait of the guy in the ground-floor foyer. That portrait was the target of much teasing and admiring female comment. Why? Dionysios Alexiakis was drop-dead gorgeous. Dionysios Alexiakis, popularly known as Dio, the ruthless, asset-stripping Greek billionaire who ran Alexiakis International. Oh, dear heaven, she registered sickly, she'd picked the wrong set of double doors to intrude behind. Now both her job *and* Meg's had to be on the line!

A grey-haired older man appeared from behind Dio Alexiakis. Frowning at her in dismay, he dug out a mobile phone. 'She's not the regular cleaner, Dio. I'll get onto security straight away.'

'There's no need for that,' Ellie protested through teeth that were starting to chatter. 'I'm just covering for the usual cleaner tonight…that's all. I'm sorry. I didn't mean to interrupt you…I was just about to step back outside—'

'But you had no business being here in the first place,' the older man condemned.

Dio Alexiakis studied her broodingly, eyes so dark they glittered like reflective mirrors and unnerved her. 'She was hiding behind the door, Millar.'

'Look, it may have *looked* like I was hiding behind the door,' Ellie argued in growing desperation. 'But why would I be hiding? Does that make sense? I'm just a cleaner. I can see I made a mistake coming in here, and I'm really sorry. I'll get out right now—'

Without warning, a large brown hand stretched out to close round her narrow wrist and halt her backward drift towards the door. 'You're not going anywhere. What's your name?'

'Ellie…I mean, Eleanor Morgan…what are you *doing*?' she gasped.

But it was too late. Dio Alexiakis had already tugged loose the scarf she had tied round her head. Her silvery pale hair fell round her shoulders in tumbled disarray. He towered over her, easily six foot three. Feeling menaced by his sheer size, Ellie gazed up at him, green eyes locking into fathomless black.

Her tummy clenched as if she had dropped from a height, the oddest sensation of dizziness making her head swim and her knees tremble. His frowning appraisal had become an outright smouldering stare of sexual assessment.

'You don't look like any cleaner I've ever met,' he finally breathed in a roughened, accented undertone.

'You meet a lot?' Ellie heard herself ask foolishly, but then she had been thrown way off balance by what she had seen in his eyes. That age-old oversexed male to female reaction she despised.

'Ellie...there *is* an Eleanor Morgan on the maintenance roster,' the older man he had referred to as Millar cut in flatly. 'But she's supposed to be working on level eight, and Security haven't cleared her for this floor. I'll have her supervisor sent up to identify her.'

As the other man relayed that information, the Greek tycoon's hard, dark features tautened. '*No. Get off that phone now. The fewer people who know about this intrusion the better.*' Releasing her wrist, he stepped back to swing out a swivel chair. 'Take a seat, Ellie.'

'But I—'

'*Sit!*' he emphasised, as if he was dealing with a puppy in dire need of basic training.

Her teeth locking together at that style of address, Ellie dropped down, her slim back rigid but her heartbeat still racing. So she had walked in where she shouldn't have. She had apologised. In fact she had all but grovelled, she reflected resentfully. So why the continuing fuss?

'Perhaps you'd care to explain what you're doing on this floor? Why you came into this particular office and why you chose to stay and eavesdrop behind a door?' Dio Alexiakis spelt out with harsh exactitude.

The silence simmered. Momentarily, Ellie wondered if bursting into tears would get her off the hook. She met those hard black eyes and her heart skipped a startled beat. With Dio Alexiakis already behaving as if she had committed a criminal offence, honesty now seemed the wisest and safest course.

'I've been having a bit of a problem with this bloke who works late on level eight,' Ellie admitted with fierce reluctance.

'What sort of problem?' Millar prompted.

Dio Alexiakis let his intense dark gaze roam with bold intimacy over Ellie's small tense figure, lingering at length on the tilted thrust of her breasts defined by the overall and the slender perfection of her legs. As mortified colour ran up beneath her fair skin his wide, sensual mouth quirked. 'Look at her, Millar. Then tell me you still need an answer to that question,' he advised drily.

Still reeling resentfully from that shameless clothes-stripping appraisal, Ellie breathed jerkily. 'I mentioned the situation to the woman who normally works up here and asked if I could switch floors with her for a night. After a *lot* of persuasion, she agreed, and she did warn me not to clean the office behind the double doors...but unfortunately there are two sets of double doors—'

'So there are,' Dio Alexiakis conceded, his agreement smooth.

'I made a simple mistake, and I was about to slip out again when I heard somebody coming,' Ellie confided tautly. 'I was scared it was a security guard. He might've asked what I was doing up here, and that could have got Meg into trouble. I dived behind the door so that I wouldn't be seen. It was a stupid thing to do—'

'Security haven't been up here since six,' the older man interposed, unimpressed. 'And when Mr Alexiakis arrived just ten minutes ago this entire floor was empty.'

'Well, I don't know who it was. He stood in the doorway for about twenty seconds and then went away again...' Wondering why her reasonable explanation was being challenged, Ellie found her voice trailing away.

Expelling his breath in a slow, measured hiss, Dio Alexiakis lounged back against the edge of a nearby desk and glanced at the anxious older man. 'Go on home, Millar. I can deal with this.'

'I should stay and sort this out for you—'

'You have a dinner date to keep,' Dio reminded him drily. 'I've made you late enough as it is.'

Millar looked as if he was about to protest, and then, meeting his employer's expectant scrutiny, he nodded. Just before he took his leave, he paused to remark gruffly, 'My thoughts will be with you tomorrow, Dio.'

Dio Alexiakis tensed, his eyes veiling. 'Thank you.'

He closed the door in the older man's wake and swung back to survey Ellie.

'I'm afraid I can't trust your word on this, Ellie,' he drawled in a tone of daunting finality. 'You listened to a very confidential dialogue—'

'I wasn't listening…I wasn't interested!' Ellie told him frantically, intimidated much against her own will.

'I've got two questions for you,' Dio Alexiakis advanced softly. 'Do you want to keep your job?'

Ellie stiffened even more, despising him for using such bullying tactics. 'Of course I do—'

'And do you want the other lady who allowed you to come up here and work in her place to keep her job?'

Ellie sagged as if he had punched her, and turned very pale. 'Please don't involve Meg in this,' she argued strickenly. 'This was *my* mistake, not hers!'

'No, she chose to break the rules,' Dio Alexiakis contradicted with lethal cool. 'She's as much involved in this as you are. And if you *are* some kind of spy, in the pay of one of my competitors, you must've made it well worth her while to agree to tonight's switch.'

'A *spy*? What on earth...?' Ellie whispered unevenly, her whole attention focused on that strong, dark face.

'Right at this moment, I find your reference to another unseen and unidentifiable individual's presence rather too convenient,' Dio Alexiakis admitted bluntly. 'If there is an information leak, you have already supplied yourself with the excuse of a third party to take the heat.'

'I d-don't know what you're talking about.' He had her so much on edge that for the first time in her life Ellie couldn't think straight.

'For your sake, I hope you don't,' Dio Alexiakis conceded, with every appearance of grim sincerity. 'But you must understand that to just let you walk back out of here is too big a risk for me to take. If you shared what you heard with the wrong person it could seriously damage my plans.'

'But I wouldn't dream of repeating what I heard!'

'So you *do* remember what you overheard. And yet only a minute ago you swore that you weren't even interested enough to *listen*!'

At that silken reminder, a frank look of dismay leapt into Ellie's eyes. She stared back at him with a sinking heart. She did have perfect recall of what he had said, but had intended to play dumb and keep that news to herself. However, he had tied her in verbal knots and tripped her up. He had a mind like a steel trap, she conceded furiously. Keen, suspicious, quick and deadly in its accuracy.

Dio Alexiakis glanced at the slim gold watch on his wrist and then back at her. 'Allow me to show you the bigger picture here, Ellie. As long as this deal goes down on Wednesday, you and your foolish friend will still be gainfully employed in this building. But until Wednesday comes, you're not moving out of my sight!'

'I b-beg your pardon?'

'Naturally, I'll pay you well for the inconvenience—'

'Inconvenience?' Ellie interrupted in a hopelessly squeaky voice.

'I assume you have a passport?'

'A *passport*? Why are you asking me that?' she gasped.

'I have to fly to Greece tonight. Keeping you under surveillance to ensure that you make no phone calls will require you to fly to Greece with me,' he delivered with perceptible impatience.

'Are you absolutely mad?' Ellie mumbled shakily.

'Do you live alone or with your family?' he questioned.

Transfixed by her own bewilderment, Ellie muttered, 'Alone, *but*—'

'A winged ebony brow rose at that news, black eyes briefly welding to her beautiful face. 'You surprise me. Where do you keep your passport at home?'

'In my bedside cabinet, but *why*—?'

Dio Alexiakis punched out a number on his mobile phone. 'I don't see any alternative to a trip to Greece,' he informed her in a sardonic aside. 'I could lock you up without a phone, but I think you'd be even less happy with that option. And I can hardly ask my household staff here in London to keep you imprisoned while I'm out of the country! You *have* to accompany me of your own free will.'

Free will? What free will? Ellie's lower lip finally dropped away from her upper as she appreciated that he was deadly serious. In the simmering silence she listened to him talk at some length on the phone in what she assumed to be Greek, his tone brusque, commanding. She heard her own name mentioned and tensed up even more.

'But I…I *swear* I won't tell anyone a word of what I heard!' she protested feverishly as he came off the phone again.

'Not good enough. By the way, I've just instructed one of my staff to open your staff locker in the maintenance department and extract your keys.'

'You've *what*?' Ellie flew upright, angry colour lighting her cheeks.

'Your address is in your personnel file. Demitrios will pick up your passport and bring it to the airport.'

Eyes wide with incredulity, Ellie snapped, 'I don't think so…I'm going home right now!'

'Are you? It really is do or die time, Ellie,' Dio Alexiakis advanced with a measuring look of challenge. 'You *can* walk out through that door. I can't stop you. But I can sack both you and your friend, and believe me, if you walk out, I *will!*'

Halfway to the door, Ellie stilled with a jerk.

'I think it would be much more sensible for you to accept the inevitable and come along quietly. That is, assuming you're the innocent party you say you are,' he completed softly, studying her with brilliant black questioning eyes.

'This is crazy! Why would I risk my job by telling anyone what I overheard?' Ellie demanded starkly.

'That information could sell for a great deal of money. I think that would supply sufficient motivation.' Dio Alexiakis strode to the threshold of the inner office he had emerged from earlier. 'Are you coming?'

'Coming where?' Ellie muttered.

'I have a helicopter waiting on the roof. It'll take us to the airport.'

'Oh...' He might as well have admitted to having a dinosaur waiting on the roof. She could not have been more taken aback. 'A helicopter?' she repeated weakly.

Seeming finally to appreciate that she was para-lysed by sheer disbelief at what he was calmly de-manding of her, Dio Alexiakis strode back across the room, closed a powerful hand over hers and urged her in the direction he wanted her to go. Pausing only to lift a heavy dark overcoat off a chair-arm, he hurried her across a palatial office with huge corner windows and pressed her through a door on the far side of the room.

'This can't be happening to me,' Ellie whispered dazedly as she stumbled up a flight of steps.

'That wish cuts both ways,' he drawled curtly from behind her. 'I have no desire for company on this particular trip.'

As he reached a long arm past her to open the steel door at the top, a blast of cold spring air blew her hair back from her face and plastered her thin overall to her slight body. She shivered violently. Having already donned his overcoat, Dio Alexi-akis side-stepped her to stride towards the silver helicopter and the pilot stationed by its nose.

'Hurry up!' he shot at her over a broad shoulder.

'I haven't even got my coat!' Ellie heard herself shriek at him, losing her temper with a sudden-ness that shook her.

He stopped dead and wheeled round. With an air

of grim exasperation and quite unnecessary male drama, he began to shrug back out of his coat.

'Don't waste your time!' Ellie snapped, temper leaping even higher at that display of grudging gallantry. 'I wouldn't wear your stupid coat if I had pneumonia!'

'So freeze in silence!' Dio Alexiakis launched back at her at full throttle, black eyes flashing like forked lightning.

Ellie squared her slight shoulders. Only the frank fascination of the watching pilot persuaded her to put a lid on her anger. Quite untouched by a slashing response that would have intimidated ninety per cent of the population, and keeping her wind-stung face stiff as concrete, Ellie stalked past Dio Alexiakis and climbed gracefully into the rear seat of the helicopter.

'I'll buy you some clothes at the airport,' the abrasive Greek slung at her as he swung in beside the pilot. He turned his head towards her, putting his hard, classic profile into stark view, adding thinly, 'We'll have plenty of time to kill. Waiting for your passport to arrive will probably cost the jet its take-off slot!'

'You are so gracious,' Ellie framed in an unmistakable tone of sarcasm, and his brows drew together in disconcertion a split second before the deafening whine of the rotor blades shattered the tense silence and she turned away again.

This is not happening to me. This *cannot* be happening to me, Ellie told herself all over again as the helicopter first rose in the air and then went into a stomach-churning dip and turn to head out across London. Having employed the equivalent of blackmail, Dio Alexiakis was now set on practically kidnapping her! What choice had he given her? *No* choice! How could she possibly run the risk of getting Meg fired? The older woman didn't have the luxury of a second salary to fall back on, and her husband was disabled.

But was she herself *really* any more independent? Ellie asked herself tautly. If it had simply been a question of survival, she could have managed without her earnings as a cleaner. After all, she had a day-job as well, and a healthy savings account. In fact, Ellie lived like a church mouse, squirrelling away every penny she could, willing to make just about any sacrifice if it meant she could attain her ultimate goal.

And that goal was buying the bookshop where she had worked since she was sixteen. However, if the steady flow of savings into her bank account ceased just when she was on the brink of asking for a large business loan, her bank manager would be most unimpressed, and her ambition to own the shop she loved would suffer a serious, indeed potentially fatal setback. Right now, with her elderly boss becoming increasingly eager to sell and retire, time was of the essence.

Dio Alexiakis was paranoid, absolutely paranoid, she decided helplessly. A *spy*? Did he read a lot of thrillers? So a cleaner had accidentally entered his precious inner sanctum and overheard him discussing confidential business plans. A cleaner who didn't have permission to work on the top floor, a little voice reminded her. A cleaner who shouldn't have been there, shouldn't even have entered that office, caught sneaking out from behind a door looking guilty as hell...

OK, Ellie conceded grudgingly, so she must have looked a bit suspicious in those circumstances. But that still didn't justify his outrageous insistence that he couldn't trust her out of his sight for the next thirty-six hours. And to demand that she travel abroad with him into the bargain was, in her opinion, proof of sheer insanity!

That wasn't his *only* problem either. The way Dio Alexiakis had looked at her a couple of times had infuriated her. Even in the midst of what he had clearly seen as a very serious situation, Dio had still been eying her up like a piece of female merchandise on offer. Compressing her generous mouth into a most ungenerous line, Ellie ruminated on that fact.

Ricky Bolton had been hard enough to tolerate, refusing to take no for an answer and convinced that he only had to persist to wear her down. That she had experienced that strange sense of disorientation when Dio Alexiakis had looked down at her didn't surprise Ellie in the slightest. This arrogant Greek had merely incited a stronger sense of revulsion than even his subordinate did. But then he was one of those *very* earthy guys, she decided grimly, the sort who couldn't look at any reasonably attractive woman without wondering what she might be like in bed!

Quite impervious to Ellie's growing antipathy, which she expressed in frigid silence, Dio Alexiakis marched her through the airport to a busy shopping area. Striding straight into an exclusive boutique, he headed for a rack of lightweight black skirt suits. Dumping the smallest size available into Ellie's startled arms, he snatched a hat, purse and long black gloves down from the display shelf above and added them.

The remainder of the tastefully concocted display fell flat on the stand. Flushing to the roots of her hair beneath the aghast scrutiny of the saleswoman surging forward, Ellie whispered in a mortified undertone, 'What on earth do you think you're doing?'

'Shopping,' Dio Alexiakis delivered succinctly, quite indifferent to the staff eyes now trained on their every move.

Like a steamroller, he headed for another rack, to pull a blue cotton shift dress from a hanger and stuff it with equal unconcern into her dismayed grasp. A long black coat was thrust at her in the same careless fashion. Then he paused by a severely undersized candy-pink shorts outfit on a dummy. With an imperious inclination of his dark head, he hailed the frozen-faced older woman already moving their way. 'We'll have this as well.'

'I'm afraid that item is sold out, sir,' he was told acidly.

'Take it off the dummy, then,' Dio instructed the woman, whose badge proclaimed her managerial status.

'Mr Alexiakis!' Ellie hissed, cringing with embarrassment.

On the clear brink of making a deflating retort, the older woman's mouth fell open when she heard that name and took a better look at the tall black-haired male towering over Ellie. 'M-Mr Alexiakis?' she stammered in incredulously.

'Yes, the owner of this chain of shops,' Dio confirmed, surveying the unfortunate woman with menacing disapproval. 'Tell me, do your staff usually stand around chatting when there are customers requiring attention? And since when has a display been more important than making a sale?'

'You're quite right, sir. Please allow me to assist you,' the manageress muttered unevenly, her discomfiture unconcealed.

'This lady needs lingerie. Pick some out for us.' His attention falling on the shoe racks, he dragged Ellie across to them. 'What size are you?'

'I don't think I've ever been more embarrassed in my life.' Ellie was trembling with rage and chagrin. 'Is this the way you normally behave in public?'

'What's the matter with you?' he demanded with ringing impatience. 'We don't have time to waste. Choose some shoes.'

In the background the manageress was struggling to strip the shorts outfit from the mannequin with hands that were visibly trembling.

In a sudden move of desperation, Ellie stretched up and heaped all the garments into his arms instead. 'Why don't you just go over to the checkout and wait for me there?'

'I'll stay here to expedite matters—'

'You are *not* standing around while I choose undergarments!' Ellie hissed up at him, like a viper ready to strike, infuriated green eyes flaming bright as jewels. 'I don't need so much stuff either.'

Black eyes scorched down into hers. 'I'm paying you to do as you're told—'

'If I have to put up with you, it'll need to be plenty!'

His brilliant gaze literally shimmered, a dark flush of colour accentuating the savage slant of his sculpted cheekbones. Incredulity emanated from him in waves. *Nobody* speaks to me like that—'

'Oh, stop throwing your weight around,' Ellie told him witheringly.

'I—'

'You've behaved atrociously from the moment we walked in here,' Ellie condemned fiercely. 'Go over to the checkout and keep quiet, and try not to terrify the life out of anybody else!'

Turning her back on him, unperturbed by the rasp of Greek invective Dio Alexiakis was audibly struggling to restrain, Ellie chose a pair of high-heeled black sandals and tried them on. They fitted. She passed them to him without a backward glance before joining the ashen-pale manageress at the lingerie section and hurriedly selecting a nightdress and some sets of bras and briefs. Argument, she sensed with a shudder, might well lead to further public mortification. She would leave the clothes behind when she was finally free of the dreadful man. And already the mere thought of another thirty-six hours in Dio Alexiakis's domineering and boorish radius daunted her.

He handed the blue dress and the shoes back to her. 'Put them on,' he commanded with studied insolence.

Cheeks adorned with flags of outraged scarlet, Ellie stalked into a cubicle. He had no manners. He was incredibly confrontational, unnervingly uninhibited and outspoken. As for the way he reacted when he got a taste of his own medicine back—well, he went up in flames like a rocket! When she emerged again, the entire staff were engaged in wrapping the rest of the purchases. Never had Ellie been more grateful to leave a shop.

'I suppose you want to go in there,' Dio condemned with unconcealed exasperation as he surveyed a busy outlet which sold cosmetics and toiletries.

'No…no, I'll manage fine!' Ellie swore in haste. 'Prehistoric man cleaned his teeth with a twig. Maybe I'll pick one up somewhere on the way.'

Dio dealt her an arrested glance. And then he really shocked her. He flung back his imperious dark head and laughed with spontaneous amusement. Ellie simply gaped, heart-rate speeding up, pulses jumping. His even white teeth flashed against bronzed skin, dark, deep-set eyes gleaming with appreciation. Humour drove all brooding darkness from his lean, powerful face, leaving her bemusedly conscious of just how stunning he was in the looks department.

'I'm not into shopping,' he confided huskily, as if she might not already be aware of that reality. 'Other people usually do it for me.'

Her complexion uncomfortably warm, Ellie dragged her attention from him and studied the floor, but that Mediterranean dark and devastating face was still imprinted in her mind's eye. He really *was* spectacular. That stark acknowledgement, that very thought, seriously unsettled Ellie. Dio Alexiakis wasn't making the tiniest effort to impress or please her. Yet somehow he still made her effortlessly aware of his high-voltage male sexuality. She didn't like that sensation, didn't like the unease and tension he provoked inside her.

She might be only twenty-one, but it was over a year since Ellie had gone out on a date. Men, she had decided, were a waste of precious time and effort, and she hadn't once regretted that decision. She didn't consider herself a man-hater, but she did get a secret kick out of jokes that suggested the male sex was useless and increasingly surplus to female requirements. After all, by and large, that *had* been Ellie's experience from childhood.

As Dio urged Ellie at speed through the crowded terminal, he rested a lean hand lightly on her taut spine to keep her moving. She stiffened defensively. 'Excuse me,' she heard herself say stiltedly, stepping back, suddenly determined to escape him, even if it could only be for a little while.

'Where do you think you're going?' he demanded.

'The ladies' cloakroom,' Ellie framed with frigid emphasis. 'Are you planning to come with me?'

His aggressive jawline squared. 'I'll give you two minutes.'

Pointedly dumping the carrier bags she was loaded down with at his feet, she began to walk away.

'Ellie...' He extended a comb to her with a sardonic look. 'Maybe you should do something with your hair while you're in there.'

Gritting her teeth at the realisation that she hadn't taken the time to check her appearance in the shop, and strongly resisting an unusually feminine urge to start smoothing her hair down, Ellie vanished into the cloakroom.

It was the work of a moment to tame her bright hair back into a straight heavy fall just below her shoulders. She frowned at her reflection, noticing the animated pink in her cheeks, the surprising sparkle in her eyes. The dress had a cool simplicity she liked, but it wasn't her style.

Her full pink mouth tightening, Ellie studied the expensive silver comb he had given her and recalled the ease with which he had accurately assessed her dress size. But then that had not been a surprise to her. At twenty-nine years of age, Dio Alexiakis was an unrepentant, totally unreconstructed womaniser. Naturally he was, Ellie reflected cynically. Men with money and power lived in a buyers' market of all too willing women. Dio was a real babe magnet, and he *knew* it. He had undoubtedly never had to worry too much about honing the rough edges from his less than presentable manners.

But, even so, she was to get a free trip to Greece. Private jet, five-star luxury all the way. The drawback? Dio Alexiakis breathing down her neck. An adventure, she told herself staunchly. Even with *him* around it ought to be more fun than polishing endless floors.

Heavens, she realised abruptly, she'd have to ring Mr Barry. Tomorrow morning her boss would be expecting her to open up as usual. He never turned in until noon, and when he found the shop still locked up he'd go straight upstairs to her bedsit and hammer on the door, thinking she had fallen ill. Regardless of Dio's embargo, she *had* to phone Mr Barry, and as she could hardly tell the older man the truth, she would have to lie to excuse her absence.

Carefully concealing herself behind a pair of large, gossiping women, Ellie slipped out of the cloakroom and lunged breathlessly at the public phone only a few yards away. Dio Alexiakis was now standing in the centre of the busy concourse, talking on his mobile phone, his attention conveniently distracted.

Ellie dialled the operator. Since she had no cash on her at all, she would have to request a reverse-charge call. But just as the operator answered, Dio turned his dark, arrogant head. She crashed the receiver back on the hook, but she wasn't quick enough. Dio saw her before she could put some space between herself and the phone.

Ellie froze like a criminal as glittering black eyes locked to her in instantaneous judgement, his lean, strong face darkening as he strode towards her. And Ellie, who knew all too well what it felt like to be irritated or bored by a member of the male sex, discovered for the first time in her life what it felt like to be *scared*...

CHAPTER TWO

EYES as dangerous as black ice scanned Ellie's pale face. 'The instant I allowed you out of my sight, you rushed to the phone to pass on the information you overheard. You have betrayed my trust!' Dio Alexiakis condemned with scantily suppressed savagery.

Even trembling, and with her stomach knotted light with apprehension, Ellie was fascinated by the volatile charge of that explosive Mediterranean temperament and that innate sense of drama. Both were so utterly foreign to her.

'Mr. Alexiakis—' she began, keen to disabuse him of his eagerness to assume the worst.

'You have made your choice. So be it.' Dio surveyed her with cold, lethal menace. 'I will destroy you for this.'

Ellie's tummy performed an unpleasant somersault. 'You've got it wrong,' she protested feverishly. 'I only got as far as dialling the operator!'

With a look of thunderous derision, Dio swung

on his heel and strode away, outrage etched in every line of his lean, tight, powerful body.

For an instant, disconcertion froze Ellie to the spot. Oh, yeah, just drag me out to the airport on your stupid helicopter and then dump me with no money and a very nasty threat! Only unfreezing as fear for her co-worker Meg's future job security assailed her, Ellie raced after Dio Alexiakis, hating him like poison.

'Get out of my way,' he growled when she got in front of him.

'That call I was trying to make wasn't what you thought it was either!' Ellie argued hotly.

He simply side-stepped her.

'You are so *stubborn*!' Ellie flung wrathfully in his wake. 'All I did was try to make a reverse-charge call to my boss at the bookshop...all right?'

Stilling, Dio swung back with stormy reluctance. 'What bookshop?' he ground out.

Ellie stared at him with a frown, sensing something missing, and then she exclaimed, 'What the heck have you done with the bags? For goodness' sake, you just walked off and left them lying on the floor, didn't you?'

Ellie went into automatic reverse, spinning round to retrace his steps. Her attention settled on the abandoned carrier bags with relief. Hurrying back, she grabbed them up.

'What bookshop?' Dio repeated stonily when she'd made it back to his side, laden like a pack-horse.

'I work in one during the day. I also live above the shop...' Ellie paused to get her breath back. 'I *have* to contact Mr Barry to warn him that I'll be taking time off. He'll call the police if I suddenly vanish—'

'Rubbish! He'll assume that you've taken off with some boyfriend. Staff of your age are often unreliable,' Dio Alexiakis asserted, unimpressed.

Affronted by the response, Ellie breathed in very deep to control her temper, but it didn't work.

'You know, I've had it up to here with you!' she told him bluntly, tipping back her silvery fair head to survey him with angry resentment. 'I do not have a boyfriend and I am *not* unreliable. Don't underestimate me and don't talk down to me, Mr Alexiakis. I always turn in for work. I've been in the same job for five years, and for the past two I've virtually been running the business—'

'So what are you doing slogging as a cleaner five nights a week?' he incised drily.

'I need the money…OK?' she flared. 'Is that really any of your business?'

'Your insolence outrages me.' Shimmering dark, deep-set eyes raked over her, the lean, bronzed features hard as steel.

'So I don't like you…what do you expect? I haven't done anything wrong. I made a silly mistake, but it's being treated like a major crime!' Ellie recounted in an accusing undertone. 'You're blackmailing me into doing what I don't want to do…and I don't appreciate your conviction that because I'm poor I'm more likely to be dishonest!'

'Are you quite finished?'

Feeling as if she had run smash-bang into a brick wall and bruised herself all over, Ellie reddened and compressed her lips.

'Today of all days,' he breathed with harsh emphasis, 'I am not in the mood for this nonsense. Come on. We have wasted enough time.'

'You believe me, then…?' Ellie prompted a minute or two later as she struggled to keep up with his long, powerful stride.

'All I believe is that I caught you *before* you contrived to disobey my explicit warning not to telephone anyone,' Dio contradicted with succinct bite. 'You're little *and* sneaky. Why does that not surprise me?'

'I am not sneaky!'

'You could have explained that you had another employer. I'm not an unreasonable man,' Dio stated grimly. 'But you chose to sneak instead of being open and honest.'

If he said 'sneak' again, she swore she would slap him. Her cheeks flamed, but the threat of thirty lashes at dawn wouldn't have dragged an apology from her. Asking him permission to do anything would have choked her. And, whether he liked it or not, that call to Mr Barry still had to be made. Unfortunately the prospect of telling little white lies to Mr Barry in Dio Alexiakis's presence made her squirm.

Ellie didn't make a habit of lying. If anything, she tended to be too honest, too blunt. She knew her own failing well, but some of her failings were also her strengths. She was fiercely independent and had never been a team player. She loved having the freedom to make her own decisions. As a result, both her jobs suited her perfectly. She preferred to work alone and without interference.

Almost an hour later, when Dio's brooding silence was fraying her nerves, her passport and her keys were handed over at a prearranged meeting point by an older man in a dark suit, whom Dio called Demitrios. Both men totally ignored her, and talked for what felt like a very long time in Greek.

'I hope you didn't leave my place in a mess,' Ellie finally remarked, rather loudly.

When she spoke, Demitrios frowned in complete surprise, much as if a suitcase had suddenly opened its mouth and tried to chat.

'And I hope you locked up properly again.' At that point a strangled groan erupted from Ellie. 'For goodness' sake, how the heck did you get past the alarm system in the first place? And did you *reset* the—?'

'My security staff are not stupid,' Dio interposed crushingly, openly aggravated by her interruptions. 'The premises will have been left in order.'

Ellie tilted her chin. 'It must be comforting to know that you have staff who can trespass as efficiently as burglars.'

Dio dealt her a thunderous glance from brilliant black eyes.

'It's rude to ignore people,' she told him stubbornly, and spun away.

But then you're just a cleaner, she reminded herself in exasperation. The lowest of the low in any staff hierarchy. Even worse, she was stuck with a guy used to being waited on hand and foot by servants. Behaving as if she was the invisible woman didn't tax Dio in the slightest. He expected her to maintain a respectful silence unless first invited to speak. But she had never been that good at keeping her tongue between her teeth, she acknowledged ruefully.

Feeling cold now that she was no longer being kept warm by carting heavy bags around, not to mention the need to walk at about five times her natural speed, Ellie took out the black coat, ripped off the sale label and put it on. The hem hit the floor. If she pulled up the collar she would look like a small moving blanket.

'Here…' Dio Alexiakis extended his mobile phone to her.

Ellie blinked in complete disconcertion.

'Your story checks out. Demitrios confirms it. You may call the owner of the bookshop.'

Ellie punched out the number. As soon as he heard her voice, Mr Barry asked anxiously if something had happened at the shop. Reassuring him, but resentfully conscious of Dio listening to every word, she explained that she would be off work for a couple of days, and apologised for the lack of warning she was giving him. She said a close friend was ill.

Ending the call with relief, she returned the phone to Dio Alexiakis.

He shot her a grim, measuring look. 'You're a very convincing liar.'

Several hours later, Ellie was appreciatively conceding that the interior of the Alexiakis private jet was something else.

Her eyes roved with keen curiosity in every direction. Opulent cream leather seating, plush carpet and elegant dcor. The cabin was far more like a luxurious reception room than mere passenger space. And did Dio Alexiakis realise how lucky he was? Did he heck!

Ellie surveyed her reluctant host. While they had waited endlessly at the airport for a fresh take-off slot for the jet he had paced the VIP lounge, exuding frustration and wrathful impatience in enervating waves. Now they were finally airborne, but from what she could see he was in no better a mood.

Even so, she still found herself studying him. The dense blue-black hair so perfectly styled to his well-shaped head. The spectacular eyes enhanced by luxuriant ebony lashes. Eyes the colour of midnight that could glint like diamond stars. The hard planes and hollows of his fabulous bone structure. Strong cheekbones added character. His arrogant nose gave warning. And that wide, perfect mouth? Passion and sensuality. She pondered on the mystery of how a particular set of features could add up to such a devastating whole.

And by the time she surprised herself at that stage, she'd got distinctly hot and bothered, and acknowledged a truth she would sooner have denied. She fancied the socks off Dio Alexiakis! Who had she been trying to kid when she'd told herself he revolted her? But it had been such a very long time since Ellie had been physically attracted to a man that she was sincerely stunned by the revelation. Just hormones playing a trick on her to remind her that she could be as foolish and fallible as any other woman, she told herself. Urgently.

But even in a filthy mood, Dio Alexiakis *was* incredibly sexy. If she had noticed, he *had* to be! Possessed of that rare fluidity of a male totally in touch with his own body, he moved like a big cat prowling on velvet paws. And he was beautifully built. Broad shoulders, taut, flat stomach, slim hips, long, lean powerful thighs, she assessed, taking individual note of each attribute. *Fantasy man*...well, until he opened his mouth, she conceded, or left her carting the bags, or looked through her with supreme disdain while never once enquiring if she was hungry or thirsty. Not a feeling guy. Tough, selfish, single-minded and utterly ruthless in attaining his own ends...

Caught staring, Ellie clashed in shock with Dio's narrowed intent gaze. Eyes that could turn to the glowing gold of topaz in sunlight, she registered, suddenly running alarmingly short of breath. But it was a kind of alarm new to Ellie's experience. Edge-of-the-seat excitement, she labelled in disbelief, finding it impossible to break free of that smouldering golden appraisal. Feverish tension held her fast, the thunder of her accelerated heartbeat pounding in her ears like surf as her mouth ran dry. An arrow of twisting heat coiled up through her and warm colour stained her face.

'It's three in the morning Greek time. You should lie down for a while and try and get some sleep,' Dio murmured thickly.

The very sound of that deep, dark drawl was like honey drenching her every straining sense, sending a delicious little shiver through her taut frame.

Ellie blinked like a sleepwalker waking up. 'Lie down?' she mumbled.

A dark line of blood now accentuated the hard arc of his cheekbones. He reached out and pressed a service button. His astonishing eyes were semi-veiled by his lush lashes. The raw tension churning up the atmosphere turned her stomach over. Complete bewilderment assailed her, followed by a sudden stark flood of intense embarrassment.

As Ellie rose jerkily upright, looking everywhere but at Dio Alexiakis, the female flight attendant appeared. Ellie was shown into a sleeping compartment. She sank down on the edge of the surprisingly large bed, powerfully disconcerted by the lingering ache in her swollen breasts and the still urgent tautness of her nipples. Never before had a man simply looked at Ellie and made her feel a hunger so powerful it hurt. But Dio Alexiakis had.

Ellie was shattered by that discovery, and ashamed of a physical reaction she had been quite unable to control. Had *he* realised what was happening to her? Had *he* recognised the effect he was having on her? She shut her eyes tight. She was appalled by the suspicion that Dio had not only recognised her helpless sexual response to him but banished her from his sight because of it.

* * *

A couple of hours later, a quiet but insistent voice roused Ellie from her uneasy doze. 'Miss Morgan…?'

Ellie came up slowly on one elbow. The flight attendant was hovering with a tray and a look of uncertainty. Ellie reached up with a grateful smile to accept the food finally being offered to her. 'Thanks…yes?'

'We…well, the cabin staff wondered if perhaps *you* would like to wake Mr Alexiakis,' she confided tautly. 'We'll be landing in fifty minutes, and naturally we're all anxious not to intrude any more than we have to—'

'Intrude?' Ellie queried, all at sea and wondering why on earth such a strange request should be made of her. Was Dio a grizzly bear when he was woken up? Had she qualified for the short straw? Did she look like cannon fodder?

The other woman sighed. 'Someone has to wake Mr Alexiakis up now so that he can dress for the funeral.'

'The funeral…' Ellie echoed, her voice just fading out altogether.

'I'm afraid this flight is very late, Miss Morgan. The delay back in London and the further delay in landing means that you'll have to travel to the funeral direct. I hope you won't think I'm being too personal, but we all think it's wonderful that Mr Alexiakis has brought someone with him for support,' she shared, and slipped out again.

Fully awakened now by sheer horror, Ellie stared into space. Oh, dear heaven, Dio Alexiakis was flying out to Greece to attend a funeral! That was why he had bought her all that black clothing! And the cabin staff had decided that she had to be somebody important in Dio's life because she was accompanying him. She remembered him saying that he hadn't wanted company on this particular trip, and groaned out loud at the memory while wondering whose funeral it was. Obviously somebody close. A relative? A dear friend?

After hurriedly choking down the breakfast on the tray, Ellie got up and rushed into the compact bathroom. She would have loved to take advantage of the shower but there wasn't time. She took out the black suit and put it on.

Her appearance in that suit astonished her. The light jacket fitted like a glove, nipping in at her tiny waist, hugging her slim shoulders, the deep vee-neck moulding her full breasts. The narrow skirt outlined the all-female curve of her hips and then tightened to outline her slender thighs. She looked sensational, she registered in amazement. Then, reddening at a vanity that seemed inappropriate, she turned from the mirror, irritated with herself for being so superficial.

Returning to the cabin, she saw Dio's impossibly long and powerful length sprawled at a most uncomfortable angle across one of the fancy leather seats. Her now tenderised and conscience-stricken heart smote her.

Shorn of his formal jacket and tie, his silk shirt open at his strong brown throat and his jawline darkly shadowed by stubble, he looked so much younger and less intimidating. He also looked absolutely exhausted, and if it hadn't been for her presence he would naturally have enjoyed the comfort of his own bed.

Ellie tensed even more. To think the cabin staff had clearly been nervous of intruding on his grief! She herself had done nothing *but* intrude! Recalling every angry combative word she had slung at the airport, Ellie cringed with guilt and shame. So the poor guy had been in a rough mood. In the circumstances, that was hardly a surprise, and his preoccupation had been equally understandable.

With a gentle hand on his shoulder, she shook him awake. His incredibly long lashes lifted off his

flushed cheekbones, and with a soft sigh, he lifted
his tousled head to check his watch. With a stifled
expletive, he then plunged forcefully upright and
headed for the sleeping compartment.

'Mr Alexiakis…?'

He stilled, but he didn't turn round.

'I didn't know you were attending a funeral,'
Ellie said awkwardly. 'I wish somebody had mentioned it.'

He swung back, frowning at her in genuine surprise. 'Don't you read newspapers?'

'I don't get time to read them.'

'It's my father's funeral,' he responded curtly,
and strode away.

Ellie slowly breathed in deep, but it didn't make
her *feel* any better. His father! What could be
worse? Of course he hadn't wanted to be lum-
bered with a total stranger over the next couple of
days. So why on earth had he insisted that she had
to accompany him?

Those extremely confidential business plans he
was so fired up about, this pretending to be interested in one company while really being interested in another, she recalled in exasperation. She
wished she understood how that information could
be as hugely important as *he* seemed to think it

was. A spy, she thought afresh, shaking her head in wonderment. Cops and robbers. Thriller territory. Way beyond anything she could even imagine.

But then Dio Alexiakis lived in a gilded world of immense wealth and privilege. He wheeled and dealed in incredibly high-powered circles. Even the night before his own father's funeral he had still been talking business. Had it been a very sudden death? Whatever, on reflection, Ellie was surprised that he hadn't already been in Greece. Even before she had entered the equation and complicated matters, hadn't he been cutting things a bit fine?

It was after seven in the morning and a bright and beautiful day when Dio Alexiakis and Ellie finally walked into Athens airport.

Wearing the suit combined with the long dramatic gloves, the extravagant-brimmed hat and the designer sunglasses which Dio had given her, Ellie felt as if she was taking part in a fancy dress parade. They were waved on by grave-faced officials. But as they passed through the barriers a wave of shouting men with cameras surged forward, held at bay only by a squad of equally determined security guards.

Ellie just froze in the glare of flashing cameras. Dio closed a powerful arm round her and carried her on through the crush as if it wasn't there, impervious to the questions being thrown in several different languages.

'Who's the woman?' she heard a man roar loudly in English.

Ellie was unnerved by the aggressive behaviour of the paparazzi. Dio was coming home to his father's funeral. What had happened to privacy? The giving of a little respectful space? For goodness' sake, was Dio hounded like this everywhere he went? Ellie hadn't the slightest idea.

But during breaks in evening shifts she had frequently heard her co-workers discussing Dio's private life in the most lurid of terms. He lived in the fast lane. He featured in glossy magazines and made endless gossip column headlines. Having enjoyed affairs with a string of gorgeous, high-profile women, he was a real sex god to the cleaning staff. But Ellie had always felt rather superior during those sessions. She hadn't had the slightest interest in the exploits of a male she neither knew nor ever expected to meet. So she hadn't listened any further.

They changed terminals and ended up in a small,

plainly furnished waiting room. Ellie was still trembling. 'Is it always like that for you?'

Dio shrugged a broad shoulder. Dark, deep-set awesomely beautiful eyes briefly touched her. 'Yes...but I'm afraid I overlooked the more extreme interest your presence would excite.'

'I hope to heaven I'm not going to be recognisable in any of those photos,' Ellie confided tautly.

Dio said nothing.

'What are we waiting for now?'

'A flight out to the island where the burial will take place.'

Another flight. She suppressed a groan. The journey seemed endless. 'The island?' she queried.

'Chindos. You really do know nothing about me,' Dio remarked with a slight frown. 'I'm not used to that.'

'But I bet it's good for you...puts a dent in your belief that you are the sun around which the entire world must turn,' Ellie muttered, and then froze in dismay. She grimaced. 'I'm sorry, I'm sorry. I was just thinking out loud!'

'That disastrous lack of tact must get you into trouble.' Dio surveyed her with a shadowy suspicion of a smile momentarily softening the hard line of his expressive mouth.

Ellie swallowed hard, grateful he hadn't exploded. 'It's been known.'

'Why are you always in search of a fight?' Dio scanned her with penetrating eyes that tightened her very skin over her bones and made her shift uneasily on her seat. 'You look so wonderfully feminine and delicate—'

Ellie winced. 'Not delicate…*please*!'

'Cute?'

'Worse,' she censured without hesitation. 'Men refuse to take me seriously. It's a big drawback being small and blonde—'

'But you're not blonde. Your hair is the colour of platinum. It's extremely eye-catching,' Dio informed her with definitive derision and the distinct air of a male unimpressed by her protest. 'If you genuinely don't want to invite that type of male attitude, you shouldn't dye it that shade.'

Ellie dealt him the weary glance of a woman who had heard it all before. 'My hair's natural. My grandmother was Dutch, and very fair.'

'Natural? I don't believe you. Take your hat off,' he urged, startling her.

After a moment's hesitation, Ellie did so, and flung back her head as if she was challenging him.

Her bright hair shone like heavy silver silk against the darkness of her jacket. 'You see, *not* fake.'

His black eyes flared gold and lingered on that shimmering fall. The silence set in then, thick as a sheet of solid steel. She watched him covertly from beneath her lashes. So very tall, so exotically dark, so still and silent. Sheathed in a sensationally well-cut black double-breasted suit, he looked truly amazing. Stop it, *stop it*. What's the matter with you? a shaken voice screamed inside her bemused head.

Perspiration beading her short upper lip, Ellie quivered, agonised by the awful reality that her own brain seemed to be romping out of control. In directions it had never gone in before. Even in the depths of infatuation at nineteen, with the latest and last of the users and abusers she'd seemed to attract, she hadn't felt overwhelmed and taken over, her very thoughts no longer her own. And there hadn't been this ghastly, utterly desperate sexual craving which flooded her every time she looked at Dio Alexiakis. She just could not *cope* with feeling like that around a man. It was so weak, so irrational, so humiliating...

'What's it like being a cleaner?' Dio enquired with quite staggering abruptness.

'Look, you don't have to make conversation with me.'

'It was a sincere question.'

'OK…it's very boring, repetitive and poorly paid,' Ellie told him with a touch of defiance. 'So if you're expecting me to say I'm some weirdo who gets a real high out of dusting and polishing—well, sorry to disappoint you!'

'So why are you doing it?'

'The hours suit me and I've got nobody on my back. I don't like being ordered around.'

'I noticed. You should deal with that problem and then consider the possibility of more challenging employment. But perhaps you have no training for any other sphere.'

'I've got plans of my own. I'm an ambitious woman in my own small way. I won't be polishing your floors for much longer,' Ellie told him with open mockery.

Dio studied her with hard black eyes. 'In the situation you're in, it's not a good idea to drop hints of that variety. I never joke about business, Ellie.'

'Neither do I. Business comes first and last in my life—'

'Really?'

'And you're running up quite a bill already,' Ellie informed him gently. 'You do realise that I expect you to pay me for every hour of the last twelve?'

'Naturally.'

'Double time too,' Ellie specified, tilting up her chin and ready to fight her corner. 'I take a dim view of being starved, deprived of breaks and kept up until three in the morning.'

Grudging amusement stirred in his brilliant eyes. 'You're your own worst enemy,' he murmured silkily. 'I'd have paid one hell of a lot more if you had just kept quiet.'

'I'm not greedy, and by the way, when I said I wouldn't be working in the maintenance department for much longer, I wasn't thinking about that stupid conversation I overheard,' Ellie told him impatiently. 'I'd forgotten about that.'

'How *could* you have forgotten about it?' Dio growled in disbelief.

'Even if I did understand the importance of what you said in that office—which I don't—I'm an honest person and I wouldn't take advantage.'

'Those who stress how honest they are, are almost always lying in their teeth,' Dio countered crushingly.

Feeling oddly hurt that his barriers had gone up again, Ellie felt her beautiful face stiffen and flush. 'Obviously you're going to believe what you want to believe. Suit yourself!'

'You can't blame me for taking every possible precaution.'

That confident assertion filled Ellie with furious resentment. Who did he think he was kidding? Without hesitation, he had used his infinitely superior power like the weapon it was! The fact that she was endeavouring to make the best of a bad situation didn't alter that brutal reality. 'Don't you *dare* try to justify yourself!' she warned him. 'Tell it like it is. If you weren't who you are and I wasn't who I am, I wouldn't *be* here! If Meg and I didn't need our jobs, I would have told you exactly where to go—'

'I can imagine,' Dio slotted in silkily.

'And, you know, dragging me along on a trip like this…well, it's not exactly a dream treat, is it? No offence or disrespect intended, but I'm not heavily into funerals,' Ellie confided.

A disconcerting flare of amusement lit Dio's steady scrutiny. 'My father would have adored your irreverence!'

Her full mouth softened. 'Was he one of the good guys?'

All his tension returned, his amusement fading as quickly as it had come. In silence, he slowly nodded, bronzed features setting hard. He swung away and she wished she had kept her stupid, clumsy mouth closed. Just for a little while he had emerged from his brooding reserve and contrived to forget what lay ahead of him.

A knock sounded on the door. It was time to move on again. Under the growing heat of the sun they walked out across the tarmac to board a small plane. A dream treat? Ellie cringed at the recollection. How could she have been that tactless? Now he was wishing she would vanish again! So why should it bother her that he felt like that? After all, how did she expect him to feel?

The plane flew out over the gleaming waters of the Aegean. In a silence filled only with monotonous engine noise, Ellie's eyes grew heavier and heavier. She sank down lower in her seat and slid into a deep, dreamless sleep.

Feeling incredibly languid, Ellie took her time about waking up again. But she frowned in sleepy disorientation when she finally focused on her surroundings. She was lying on the capacious back seat of an enormous limousine with tinted windows.

With a thick, expensive metal clunk, the passenger door opened. A black-haired young man backed by bright golden sunlight gaze down at her with patronising amusement. 'So you're Dio's latest woman… I've got to hand it to my cousin. He's got taste. No wonder he kept you out of the church. Some of his late mother's relatives are pretty narrow-minded. I'm Lukas Varios.'

Tensing with annoyance under the earthy glide of the eyes trailing over the slender length of her exposed legs, Ellie pulled herself hurriedly upright and tugged down the skirt which had ridden up while she slept. 'I am *not* Dio's woman!' she snapped.

'Nice to have a piece of good news today.' With a cocky grin on his handsome face, Lukas Varios slid in beside her and closed the door. 'So, if you don't belong to Dio, what are you doing waiting outside the cemetery for him?'

Ellie compressed her ripe pink mouth into a rigid line. 'I just work for him…OK?'

'Oh, it's *very* much OK with me…' Impervious to her frozen expression, Lukas stretched out a confident hand to finger the silvery fall of hair lying against her flushed cheekbone and murmured, 'You are a real babe—'

The passenger door opened again, this time framing Dio. He took one look at the apparently intimate scene he had interrupted and smouldering fury blazed in his spectacular eyes. He reached in a powerful hand, closed it over the younger man's shoulder and hauled him out of the limo to shoot a raw flood of guttural Greek down at him.

Lukas Varios backed off, struggling to reassert his cool by smoothing down his jacket, but his shaken face was red as fire. As Ellie sat there, immobilised by sheer shock at Dio's extraordinary behaviour, Lukas sent her a fiercely accusing glance. 'She said she wasn't yours...do you think I'd have come on to her if she'd told me the truth?'

Lean, strong face cold and hard as bronze, Dio swung into the limo and slammed the door without another word. Black contemptuous eyes flamed over Ellie. 'I didn't bring you here to behave like a tramp!' he told her with splintering derision.

CHAPTER THREE

ELLIE'S quick temper, already taxed to its limits by Lukas's offensive familiarity, simply erupted.

Reacting on instinct alone, her hand flew up and she slapped Dio Alexiakis so hard across one cheekbone her fingers stung like mad. 'No man calls me a tramp!' she bit out in furious condemnation.

As the livid marks of that slap sprang up across one slashing cheekbone, Dio stared back at her with truly stunned black eyes.

Even though Ellie instantly knew that she had gone too far, she was far too angry to acknowledge her mistake. 'And your conceited mega-ego of a cousin deserves the same!' she launched in defiant addition. 'Who does that little squirt think he is? Calling me a *babe*, and smirking and pawing my hair like I'm some kind of toy to be played with! And how dare you behave in such a way as to give him the impression that I would stoop to be something as utterly disgusting as *your* woman?'

'Disgusting...?' Dio gritted, not quite levelly, eyes now as scorching a gold as the heart of a bonfire.

'Yes, disgusting!' Ellie repeated with a feeling shudder. 'Women do not belong like objects to men—'

'I could persuade you to belong to me,' Dio declared in a wrathful growl.

Ellie breathed in so deep on that staggering claim she was vaguely surprised that she didn't explode. She studied him with scornful green eyes. 'What with? A Stone Age hammer? Because let me tell you, knocking me out and dragging me by force back to the family cave would be the only way!'

Without the slightest warning, Dio reached for her with powerful hands that brooked no refusal. He brought his mouth crashing down hard on hers. Shock paralysed Ellie. But a far deeper level of shock awaited her. When that wide, sensual mouth possessed hers with hungry force, it was as if the world came to a sudden screeching halt and sent her flying off into the sun.

The surge of heat Dio ignited could have burned up an entire planet. Ellie's head swam, all rational thought suspended beneath that shattering shower of instant sensation. As he hauled her into a crushing and deeply satisfying embrace, her blood pounded madly through her pliant body.

He tasted like water after a long summer drought. He created a thirst she had never known she had. She was so hooked on that electrifying excitement that she clung like a vine to a tree, moaning low in her throat as his tongue invaded the moist sensitivity of her mouth in an erotic invasion that drove her wild.

Dio dragged her back from him, his breathing fractured, his eyes blazing over her with a primitive satisfaction he couldn't hide. 'I wouldn't need to use force with you, Ellie. You'd come back to the family cave like a little lamb,' he contended thickly.

As the haze of intoxicating passion evaporated, Ellie gazed up into his darkly handsome features, aghast. Simultaneously, Dio stiffened, veiled his eyes and set her back from him. A boiling wave of hot embarrassment enveloped Ellie. She couldn't believe that what had happened had happened. She couldn't believe that she could possibly have felt what he had made her feel when she hadn't wanted to feel anything. And the silence lay there, thick and treacherous as a swamp that neither of them wanted to risk trying to cross.

'I...I...' Ellie began unevenly, suddenly eager to give both of them an acceptable excuse. 'I shouldn't have slapped you. I made you angry—'

'Greek men don't like having their masculinity challenged.' Dio loosed a sardonic laugh and dealt her a bleak glance. 'But I kissed you because I wanted to. As you said to me, tell it like it is.'

Taken aback by that blunt acknowledgement that the attraction playing havoc with her own self-discipline was not solely her problem, Ellie gazed at him in frank perplexity. Then she swiftly turned her head away.

'Naturally we won't be repeating the experiment,' Dio completed with flat finality.

Ellie's delicate profile tautened. Although he was only stating the obvious, only saying what she would have said herself, angry mortification still engulfed her. Conscious that she was being warned off, she felt humiliated. *He* had kissed *her*! Yet he still evidently saw a need to depress any foolish ideas she might be developing. Who the heck did he think he was?

Mr Totally Irresistible? *Yes*, she answered for herself. And that blazing confidence wasn't vanity, she acknowledged with driven reluctance. He had it all. The looks, the money, the power. How often did Dio Alexiakis meet with rejection? How much more often must he meet with blatant encouragement?

But still Ellie felt the need to defend herself. 'I lashed out because you were extremely ru—'

'I don't wish to discuss this any further,' Dio interposed harshly. 'I'm not myself today. My reactions are on a very short fuse.'

But in the space of a heartbeat he had blown Ellie's belief that she wasn't a very sexual person right out of the water. She could only cringe when she recalled the almost irresistible temptation to snatch him greedily back into her arms. She had never dreamt that *any* man could rouse her to that level of excitement, hunger and craving. That Dio Alexiakis had that power shook her to her very depths.

The limousine drove up the steep road at a stately crawl, other vehicles now falling in behind to follow in their wake. Above them, perched on the spectacular height of a cliff, the large domed roof of a pale building came into view. The higher they climbed, the bigger that building seemed to become. It couldn't be called a villa, Ellie decided wide-eyed, it could only be called a *palace*.

'Is this your home?' she prompted tautly.

As the limo glided to a halt in front of the massive entrance, Dio gave a bleak nod of confirmation.

'If you're going to be socialising with friends and family now, just find me a room somewhere and lock the door. I don't want to intrude—'

'You're staying with me,' Dio countered steadily.

'But what am I supposed to say if anyone speaks to me?' Ellie's dismay was unhidden. 'I don't even know what your father was called!'

'His name was Spiros. He was seventy-one and I was his only child,' Dio framed, his accent thickening to roughen his vowel sounds, his jawline squaring. 'He was one of those good guys you mentioned. He may have passed away peacefully in his sleep, but his death was both sudden *and* unexpected.'

'You had no chance to say goodbye. That's very hard to bear.' As she had listened Ellie had paled, briefly plunged into her own memories of the loss of a loved and loving parent.

Dio sent her a flashing glance of pure disdain. 'Spare me the platitudes,' he derided harshly. 'My father and I had been estranged for some time before his death.'

'It wasn't a platitude. Whose fault was it that you were…estranged?' she dared to ask.

'Mine…' She watched his lean brown hands slowly clench into powerful fists and then carefully unclench again the instant he realised she had noticed that betraying gesture.

'You couldn't have known—'

'This is none of your business!' Dio ground out thunderously.

They climbed out of the car. Ellie stole a troubled glance up at Dio's rigid profile and suppressed a rueful sigh, recognising the stoic, all-male but unnatural control he was determined to maintain. Maybe it was easier for women to let go emotionally, talk it out, forgive themselves. It was certainly wiser, she reckoned. Right now Dio Alexiakis was like a big simmering volcano, struggling to swallow back a surging lava flow. Hanging back, she let him stride ahead of her,.

A large cluster of staff were waiting in the huge, opulent entrance hall. Dio spoke a few words. Ellie hovered awkwardly in the centre of the marble floor, her attention roaming over statues in alcoves and magnificent paintings and then centring on the gorgeous brunette who had unexpectedly appeared in a doorway.

Not having noticed the other woman, Dio swung back an imperious head. 'Ellie!' he gritted impatiently.

Her colour rising as every watching eye swivelled to examine her with keen interest, Ellie quickened her step. Just as Dio clamped a large imprisoning hand over hers, the sophisticated brunette strolled forward. She looked to be in her late twenties. She had short, glossy black hair, exotic dark eyes and creamy skin. Her designer dress and her jewellery were simply breathtaking.

'Helena...' Dio drawled, his long fingers suddenly closing so tightly over Ellie's smaller hand that she almost yelped with discomfort.

Helena planted a cool kiss on his cheek and then addressed him in Greek. She ignored Ellie. But Ellie was grateful to be ignored because she was embarrassed by Dio's stubborn determination to keep her by his side. Still conversing with Helena, whom Ellie now assumed to be a close relative, Dio walked them both into a vast reception room.

Other people began to arrive. Helena took up position like a seasoned hostess. Dio's grip on Ellie's fingers had mercifully loosened, and she tried to pull away, hoping to retire to a dark corner. But not only did Dio retain his hold on her, he also swept her forward and introduced her, although nobody got the chance to engage her in any actual conversation. Many curious eyes lingered on her, but Dio kept both of them on the move. He exchanged a word here, a sentence there, his bleak, brooding tension forestalling any more intimate dialogue.

'*Cristos*...I *hate* this!' he bit out rawly under his breath at one stage.

Some minutes later, an exuberant older man grasped him in a bear hug, forcing him to release Ellie. Ellie backed away and then walked out onto the balcony that appeared to stretch the entire length of the house. She breathed in deep in the hot still air. The view out over the bay was really incredible. An endless blue sky arched over the lush, forested pine slopes sprinkled with wild flowers and the majestic rock formations that jutted out into the sparkling turquoise sea far below. It was so beautiful it almost hurt.

She stood there for a long time before she turned away again, becoming conscious of how very tired she still was. A couple of catnaps hadn't made up for the stress of a long trip and the loss of a decent night's sleep.

As she glanced back into the crowded room, she immediately noticed Dio. He was so tall he couldn't be missed. He had a dark frown on his starkly handsome features as he glanced restively around himself, only paying part attention to what was being said to him. Then his keen gaze lit like a falling star on Ellie, where she stood outside in the sun, her silver hair gleaming like precious metal. The marked strain on his lean, strong face instantly eased.

Across the distance that separated them, Ellie collided with glittering black eyes. Her heart gave a sudden violent lurch and her mouth ran dry. She watched Dio plough through the crush surrounding him. She could focus on nothing but him, and was as blind as he was to the buzz of speculation his abrupt departure had created.

'Where the hell have you been?' he breathed in a driven undertone.

But a couple of feet from her Dio ground to an equally sudden halt, an almost bemused frown pleating his winged ebony brows. Emanating megawatt tension in abundance again, he studied Ellie with ferociously intent black eyes that questioned even before he demanded, 'Why do I *want* to be with you right now?'

As tense now as he, Ellie jerked a slight shoulder in an awkward movement. 'Keeping tabs on me to ensure I don't get near a phone has b-become a real bad habit?' she stammered in a strained and breathless rush.

At that moment, Helena Teriakos strolled unhurriedly out to join them. Beneath her coolly enquiring scrutiny, Ellie found herself reddening with fierce discomfiture, although she could not have explained why.

'Miss Morgan looks quite exhausted, Dio,' the other woman commented. 'I believe she might appreciate the opportunity to retire to her room.'

'Yes…yes, I would,' Ellie agreed tautly.

The beautiful brunette awarded her a faint but dismissive smile of approval. His strong jawline clenching, Dio summoned a maid with an imperious snap of his fingers, his habit of command so ingrained in that gesture it caught Ellie's attention and made her look away.

'I'll see you later,' he informed Ellie flatly, and strode back indoors.

Why do I feel like I'm abandoning him? Ellie asked herself in genuine bewilderment as she followed the maid. Where had this ridiculous sense of connection come from? She barely knew Dio Alexiakis. She didn't even like the guy, did she? What on earth was the matter with her?

Jet lag, exhaustion, she told herself, but she knew it was more. Helpless sympathy had flared when Dio had admitted that he'd been at odds with his father before his death. She understood that he didn't feel entitled to play the grieving role of a loving son for the benefit of an audience. Yet it was patently obvious to her that he *had* been a loving son. But right now, Dio was so tormented by his conscience he couldn't see the wood for the trees.

The maid led her into a lift off the huge entrance hall. They travelled down and then traversed a corridor which took them straight back out into the open air again. Mystified, but intrigued, Ellie followed the girl down a short sloping path to a low building sited right on the edge of an endless dreamy stretch of golden sand.

The interior was wonderfully cool. It was some sort of self-contained guest suite, Ellie assumed, admiring the spacious lounge and adjoining dining area. The tall windows had elegant shutters to keep out the sun; inviting sofas adorned the marble floor. There was no kitchen, just a concealed fridge the size of a walk-in larder, packed with snacks and soft drinks. Two *en suite* bedrooms completed the accommodation. Her assorted carrier bags already sat in a rather pathetic huddle on one of the beds.

With alacrity, Ellie took the opportunity to strip off every stitch she wore and head straight for the shower. Smothering yawns, she washed, but she was conscious of the weirdest sense of dislocation. Dio drifted back into her mind, and his lean, dark, devastating image wedged there, refusing to be driven out again. She frowned in confusion.

Suddenly she remembered the way Dio had stridden towards her, and she shivered then, reluctant to examine her own response. 'Why do I *want* to be with you right now?' he had demanded, his incredulity unconcealed. Why, she should have asked herself, had she stood there waiting for him, strung out on such a high of anticipation she could hardly breathe?

That was not how Ellie acted around the opposite sex. In fact, Dio Alexiakis should already have sunk like a stone under the weight of her prejudices. Ellie thoroughly distrusted good-looking men, and was all too well aware that rich men saw women as mere trophies with which to embellish their all-important image. Her own father had been just such a man.

Only now, all of a sudden, Ellie was being forced to accept that even her most cherished convictions didn't necessarily influence how she actually behaved. Dio had spellbinding physical magnetism, but that didn't excuse her for acting like a silly little schoolgirl. In real life, Cinderella would have watched her prince waltz over the horizon and out of reach with a real princess, Ellie reflected cynically. No, she didn't see Dio Alexiakis as an essentially superior being, but in terms of cold, hard cash and status, he was as far removed from someone like her as a royal prince.

She was attracted to him, that was all, she told herself uneasily. Unfortunately that didn't explain why only self-conscious embarrassment in Helena Teriakos's presence had driven her into walking away from Dio. For after the way Dio had looked at her, exhausted or not, she had the horrendous urge to stick to him like superglue.

Donning the sheer, strappy midnight-blue nightdress because it was cool, blanking out her unproductive thoughts, Ellie padded out to the lounge again. The maid reappeared with a tray. Ellie tucked into the delicious buffet-style offerings with appetite and then curled up on a sofa, too sleepy to keep her eyes open any longer.

The arrival of yet another meal was what finally awakened Ellie, but she wasn't hungry enough to eat anything more. The sun was beginning to go down and she couldn't believe that she had slept away the entire afternoon. She would never manage to sleep again later, and what a terrible waste it had been not to at least walk along that beautiful beach outside!

She rummaged through the eclectic mix of CDs stored in the state-of-the-art entertainment centre. Smiling to herself, she put on flamenco music, remembering the endless dance and drama classes which her mother had insisted she attend. Dancing was still her favourite method of working out. She performed a few exploratory movements, letting the rhythm flow until all her muscles had loosened up. Then, picking up on the faster tempo, she gave herself up to the passionate music.

Her breasts heaving with the rapidity of her breathing, the sheer strain clinging to her damp skin, Ellie came to a fluid halt as the CD moved to an end. She let her head slowly fall back, her slender spine arching into a perfect curve.

'That was *incredible*...' Dio Alexiakis murmured with ragged emphasis.

Ellie whirled breathlessly round on her toes, the faraway look in her eyes banished by dismay and disconcertion.

Shorn of his jacket and tie, both of which trailed carelessly from one clenched hand, Dio stood in the shadows near the entrance door. He was still as a bronze statue. Then he suddenly moved an expressive hand and spread long brown fingers, the extent of his appreciation of the performance he had witnessed unconcealed.

Brilliant, dark deep-set eyes sought hers. 'Quite extraordinary,' he told her with husky intensity. 'So much fire, so much pathos, every single movement, every tiny gesture telling a story.'

As slow-burning colour swept up from her extended throat Ellie trembled, outraged that he had not immediately announced his presence. 'You should've told me you were here...you had no *right* to watch me!'

'I didn't want to interrupt you...' A shimmer of gold as bright as a flame glimmered in Dio's semi-screened gaze as it lingered on her ripe pink mouth.

Her lips parted, an alien ache stirring low in her belly as the silence stretched.

'That's not an excuse...' she protested unevenly, her slight frame tautening in instinctive reaction to the growing tension in the atmosphere.

Dio Alexiakis threw his darkly handsome head

back and surveyed her. '*Cristos*…is there a man alive who would have interrupted you?' he demanded with roughened urgency.

Ellie was so still and so tense she could feel every beat of her heart—even, she was dimly convinced, the very pulse of her blood through her veins. She collided with Dio's shimmering gaze and she felt intoxicated. Dizzy, disorientated, no longer able to get her brain to send a message to her tongue. Indeed, it was suddenly such a challenge to keep a grip on a single coherent thought that she simply stared at him in bewilderment. Her body was already responding far in advance of her brain, her breasts swelling heavily, tautened peaks pitching into almost painful prominence.

A feverish flush on his sculpted cheekbones, Dio let his stunning eyes roam hungrily over her beautiful face, and then at an incredibly slow pace over her slim figure. The fabric of the nightdress clung like a second skin to her surprisingly lush shape, moulding her straining nipples, the shapely curve of her hips and the slender line of thigh. The high-voltage charge of his powerful sexuality entrapped her, filling her with excitement and leaving her utterly without defence.

'Watching you dance was the most erotic experience I have ever had outside the bedroom door,' Dio confessed with driven urgency. 'I have never known such an overpowering need to possess a woman. And right now I'm just revelling like a crazy teenager in the pleasure of feeling something *this* intense!'

Ellie quivered, shocked rigid by that bold speech and sufficiently jarred to begin reasoning again. A crazy teenager? *Him?* What sort of a line was that? Involuntarily, she glanced down at herself and froze. Belatedly appreciating how very little she was wearing, she was quite unable to comprehend how the need to cover herself up had not been her first thought when she'd seen him!

In a stumbling surge, shorn of her usual grace, her face hot as hellfire, Ellie snatched up a throw from the nearest sofa and hauled it round herself like a screening blanket. No blooming wonder he was coming on to her! Men were not very discriminating when a woman put on a provocative display. In fact it was her belief that most men lived on the constant edge of succumbing to illicit temptation.

Dio released a soft, ruefully amused laugh. His strong features were no longer hard with tension as he scanned Ellie standing there, green eyes huge, gripping the colourful throw tightly around herself. 'Half-child, half-woman. What a confusing combination you are!'

'Stop talking like that,' Ellie urged him uncomfortably, evading his scrutiny. 'You don't know what you're saying. I'll just pretend I didn't hear what you said. I know you can't help being like that, so I'm not taking offence—'

'Perhaps this is not the moment to tell you that you have supplied the only glimmer of light in an exceedingly dark day,' Dio breathed grittily, switching mood at volatile speed as he swung with restive fluidity away from her.

'Because I'm a stranger...don't you realise that?' Ellie prompted in a voice that shook with sudden strain. She was touched against her own volition by that roughened sincerity, but eager to tell him why she believed he was acting like somebody temporarily bereft of all sanity. 'I have no expectations of you, no knowledge of your life. I don't ask anything of you. I make no judgements.'

'On the contrary, you never stop making arbitrary judgements,' Dio contradicted grimly.

'I'm going for a walk on the beach.' Shaken by the warring emotional storm beginning to make its presence felt inside her, Ellie wrenched open the door and hurriedly walked outside.

Moonlight shimmered on the sea as the surf whispered onto the shore. It was a clear night, and the air was warm and still. She trudged barefoot through the soft silky sand, fighting the turmoil he had unleashed—because she understood all too well what Dio Alexiakis was going through.

And the way Dio looked at her might scare the hell out of her on one level, but on another it electrified her. Even without him in front of her she still felt drunk. It was as if some giant, crazy infatuation had mushroomed inside her and stolen all common sense. In the space of twenty-four hours Dio had turned her inside out, dissolving her defensive shell, luring out the soft, vulnerable feelings she usually kept under lock and key.

Now that she was being honest with herself, she knew that she couldn't trust herself around him. She *wanted* Dio Alexiakis. She wanted him as she had never wanted any other man, and that alone was terrifying. But, far more dangerously, she ached to talk to him, listen to him, *be* with him…

Every alarm bell she possessed was clanging as loud as Big Ben. Dio couldn't deal with his own emotions right now so he had focused on her instead. That was the cruel reality of his supposed desire, she told herself urgently. Standard male avoidance technique. Target the nearest reasonably attractive woman and try to blot out every painful feeling with the comforting familiarity of the physical. And right now Dio Alexiakis would dance on broken glass sooner than admit his desperate need to talk about his late father.

Reaching an impulsive decision, Ellie suddenly turned in her tracks and set off back in the direction she had come. Dio was staring out to sea, both hands dug in the pockets of his well-cut trousers, his pale shirt glimmering in the shadows of the overhanging roof that shaded the entrance to the beach house.

'I bet nothing really bad has ever happened to you before,' Ellie breathed.

He swung round. 'What the hell are you talking about?'

'Did you have a happy childhood?'

'Yes!' he gritted.

'A close relationship with your father before you became estranged?'

'Of course,' Dio confirmed in a shuttered tone that would not have encouraged the wise or wary to continue.

'So why can't you just concentrate on the good times you had?' Ellie asked bluntly.

'How could *you* understand how I feel now?' he demanded with splintering aggression.

'I understand. I just don't think you appreciate how very lucky you are to have enjoyed so many years of love and support,' Ellie admitted ruefully.

Dio turned to stare at her, speechless with disbelief, his whole stance shouting his blistering anger at such a contention.

'I mean…I had a father who wouldn't even let my mother put his name on my birth certificate, a father who once walked past me in the street and pretended not to know me,' Ellie confided tightly. 'And a mother who still worshipped the ground he walked on.'

Dragged with a vengeance from his own brooding self-absorption, Dio frowned at her with frank incredulity.

'I had a major fight with my mother the day before she died,' Ellie volunteered, her throat convulsing with the sickness of tears. 'I was sixteen. I loved her so much and I was worried sick about her. I was trying to snap her out of her depression, persuade her that there was a life worth living *without* my worthless creep of a father…'

Dio had moved without her noticing. He closed two arms round her and pulled her slight, shaking body close. Dimly it occurred to her that nothing was working quite the way she had imagined it working. Then the warm, intimate scent of him drenched her senses and she breathed in deep, loving the heat and stability of his big, powerful frame.

Without the slightest hesitation, Dio was the one asking questions now. And Ellie told him about her mother. The only child of a prosperous widower, beautiful and sweet-natured Leigh Morgan had been cocooned from life's tougher realities by a parent who had idolised her. At twenty-two she had fallen in love and got engaged to Ellie's father, Tony. Then her own father had gone bankrupt and the happy days had come to an end.

'Tony didn't want Mum without her father's money,' Ellie confided. 'He broke off the engagement and not long afterwards he married the daughter of a wealthy manufacturer.'

'So he ditched your mother when she was pregnant—?'

'No, it wasn't that simple. A few weeks after he got married he went to Mum and told her that he'd made a dreadful mistake, that he still loved her. I was conceived the same day. She thought he would leave his wife.'

'Ah…' Dio murmured with expressive softness. 'But he had no such intention.'

'Mum was as green as grass and still mad about him,' Ellie conceded heavily, and then she sighed. 'I don't want to talk about them any more.'

'No problem,' Dio told her huskily, letting his big hands slide down her taut spine to curve over her hips and mould her against his lean, hard body.

'Now it's your turn…' Ellie muttered unevenly as she quivered, thought about pulling away, decided to *do* it, and then discovered that she didn't have that much will-power.

'My turn…?' Dio echoed thickly.

'Your turn,' she repeated unsteadily, a twist of heat snaking through her lower belly and tightening every tiny muscle she possessed.

'My father told me it was time I got married. I said, No, I'm not ready yet…and *he* said, "I don't want to see you or speak to you until you *are* ready,"' Dio recited with raw-edged emphasis, half under his breath.

Ellie tipped back her head to frown up at him. 'That's your joky way of telling me to mind my own business…right?'

'Wrong.'

'You mean your father just expected you to get married when *he* said so?' Ellie couldn't hide her astonishment.

'My own parents didn't just meet and date, Ellie. They knew each other from childhood, grew up knowing what was expected of them, and when the time seemed right,' Dio specified in a taut undertone, 'their fathers got together and set the wedding date.'

'For goodness' sake, that's medieval!'

'To you, perhaps. But my parents were very happy together.' Dio smoothed her tousled hair back from her damp brow with incredibly gentle fingers, making her shiver and automatically curve closer, her legs increasingly wobbly supports. 'Marriage can still be very much a family affair in Greece.'

'I don't want to criticise your father...' Ellie began hesitantly, turning the side of her face into his palm, like a sensuous cat begging to be stroked, and snatching in a fracturing breath as she struggled to concentrate. 'But I think he should've appreciated that times have changed. You're a grown man and he treated you like—'

'He knew what was best for me,' Dio slotted in

with velvet-soft finality. 'I may speak public school English, Ellie, but I *am* Greek, and marriage *is* a very serious step. The English rely on love and have a very high divorce rate—'

'Yes, *but*—'

'It's more important to pick a life partner with intelligence,' Dio stated, and then he lifted her high in his strong arms, as if he was tired of that particular subject, and sealed his sensual mouth with hungry mastery to hers.

Ellie's head spun, her heart jumping violently. He needed to talk. This wasn't what she had planned; this *wasn't* what was supposed to happen. In another minute, she swore feverishly, she would pull back, stop this before it got out of hand. But somehow her arms had got round his neck and her fingers were already sliding into the thick luxuriance of his black hair. A cloud of such debilitating weakness enveloped her that by the time she promised herself another thirty seconds she could no longer recall why that strange idea of a timeframe should come into her head.

'This was inevitable,' Dio growled, sweeping her right off her feet when she stumbled on her no longer reliable lower limbs and carrying her back into the beach house.

CHAPTER FOUR

A THOUGHT almost made it to the surface of Ellie's blank mind. And then she locked into Dio's black glittering eyes. Her heart lurched; her pulses raced. Dizzy and mindless euphoria took a hold again.

She raised an uncertain hand to cover one hard flushed cheekbone with a shy possessiveness entirely new to her. Her spread fingers rejoiced in the rougher texture of his skin, her dilated pupils searching out every tiny detail of him that close.

The lush black spiky lashes, so ridiculously long, the dramatic set of his eyes below those dark defined brows; the sheer masculine beauty of his hard bone structure; the lean, arrogant perfection of his nose. She caressed his aggressive jawline with wondering tenderness, her whole being intensely absorbed in that appraisal. Nothing had ever felt so right or so natural.

'You really are gorgeous,' she told him helplessly.

Dio brought her down on something firm and deliciously comfortable and leant over her. He stared down into her dazed eyes, his own flaming gold, and groaned, 'I thought you were the most perfect thing I ever saw in my life when I took that scarf off. Your hair, your skin, your eyes. You stunned me—'

'Guess you're s-stunning me,' Ellie stammered, wit returning to take in the fact that she was lying on a bed in a dimly lit room, sudden dismay blossoming at the edge of her euphoria.

'You're really very sweet underneath the tough front...' Dio lowered his proud dark head.

Ellie could have drowned in those topaz eyes, could literally feel weakness escaping like a honeyed dam breaking its walls inside her, sentencing her to mesmerised stillness.

He took her lips again, prying them apart with the wicked dart of his tongue. Her heart banged and her tummy quivered and she couldn't get breath back into her lungs. Her submission was absolute, instinctive. She could not have resisted the erotic allure of that kiss had her life depended on it. It was like being reborn, every sensation so sharp, so fresh, so intense she was hooked in helpless, urgent longing for the next.

'So *sweet*,' Dio growled low in his throat as Ellie

moaned and gasped under his expert mouth with shivering responsiveness.

Peeling off his shirt, he raised her to him. Ellie stiffened. The whole of her vision was filled with that broad bronzed chest and the thick, dark curling hair marking his pectoral muscles before snaking down into a fine silky furrow over his taut flat stomach. He lifted her hands and put them on him, as if it was the most natural thing in the world that she should touch him.

'Dio…' she said jerkily, shock waves running through her as the hard, hair-roughened warmth of him met her splayed fingers.

Heavens, there was so much of him, and suddenly she felt wildly out of her depth, recognising that he was encouraging and expecting an experienced partner.

'Touch me,' he invited raggedly.

She studied her own hands as if she was hoping they would lift from him without any conscious message from her brain. But he felt so fascinatingly, wonderfully good. 'This is…this is a little bit fast for me,' she mumbled with serious understatement, because she still couldn't grasp how they had got as far as undressing on a bed.

He covered her small hands with his. 'You want me to leave, I will.'

A cold stab of fear made Ellie's stomach flip. She lifted her head up to encounter sizzling dark eyes set in a lean, taut-boned face that made her ache with longing. Leave or stay. Nothing in between. And if he leaves now, maybe he'll never ask again; maybe he'll think I'm just a tease, she reflected in anguish, finally appreciating that he saw no reason why they shouldn't enjoy each other immediately.

'But I...' she began, not even knowing what she was going to say, terrified of sounding like some old-fashioned virgin and turning him off completely.

'Make your mind up.' Dio's dark drawl was urgent with stress and tension, pure, masculine need stamped on his lean dark features. 'I'm not made of steel and I am *burning* for you...'

Ellie's taut hands quivered under his. She just couldn't take her eyes off him. His intensity melted her deep down inside. 'I want you too...*so* much.'

Dio settled her gently back onto the mattress. 'I won't do anything you don't want me to do, *pethi mou*.'

'Of course not, *but*—'

'Open your mouth for me,' he urged raggedly.

And she did, taking instant fire from that passionate onslaught. She didn't notice him skimming her nightdress straps down her arms. Then he coiled back from her to remove the tangle of fabric from round her hips and she focused in shock on her own bare breasts, rising wantonly full, crested by taut pink nipples.

'You're exquisite,' Dio groaned.

Coming back to her, he let his thumb stroke a swollen bud, his palm cupping the underside of her firm breast, and then he closed his mouth there instead. He sent such a jolt of startling sensation through Ellie she cried out loud, her head falling back on the pillows, all thought suspended. Her hands gripped his smooth brown shoulders as over and over again he caressed her sensitive flesh with his tongue and his teeth and his lips. Now she was the one burning, maddened by every sure, knowing stroke, driven to a height of frantic yearning need that consumed her like a greedy fire.

Without warning Dio rolled back from her and slid off the bed backwards, burnished golden eyes welded to her pale pink body. It was like being visually consumed. She was hot and out of breath, in a state of mindless hunger beyond anything she had ever imagined possible. Her eyes followed him. She simply couldn't bear him that far away from her.

'Dio...?' she muttered uncertainly.

'You respond to me like you were made for me,' Dio told her with primal satisfaction.

She watched him unzip his well-cut pants. Her eyes widened, a shred of awareness returning. His black boxer shorts were skimmed off his lean hips a split second later. Receiving her first view of a fully aroused adult male shook Ellie. And although Dio was even more beautiful than she had naively imagined, he was considerably more intimidating. Belatedly conscious of her own nakedness, Ellie sat up and wrenched at the sheet so that she could squirm beneath its cover, her heart pounding against her breastbone as if she had run a three-minute mile.

The knowledge of her own inexperience provoked a current of panic. Dio strolled back to the bed without inhibition. In fact she doubted that Dio had ever had the slightest urge to hide himself in the bedroom. 'You're shy,' he murmured almost tenderly, but he threw back the sheet to join her, with scant allowance for that reality.

'Yes... Dio—'

'I want to look at you,' he confessed, curving her

into the hard, abrasive heat of his powerfully masculine body with a long possessive arm. 'You're shaking...'

'You're making me nervous.'

He meshed lean fingers into her thick hair and brought her mouth up to his, tasting her with deep, sensual appreciation until her head swam and the nerves were squeezed out of her by more physical reactions.

He lifted his imperious dark head then. Brilliant golden eyes gazed down into hers. 'This isn't a one-night stand. This is something exceptional and special. I don't sleep around,' he asserted with husky sincerity.

Ellie raised an unsteady hand and brushed the tousled black hair off his brow, her heart banging somewhere in the region of her throat. She couldn't believe the power he had over her. She couldn't believe that a man finally had her hanging on his every word, hoping and praying that he was worthy of her trust. It was a terrifying feeling, but when he held her eyes and touched her there wasn't a fibre of her being capable of resisting him.

Dio ran an exploring hand over her trembling length. She jerked and gasped, her whole body already so sensitised he could reawaken her with the slightest touch. When he teased the soft silver-gilt triangle at the juncture of her thighs she moaned, and thrust her burning face into his hard shoulder. With devastating expertise, he traced the hot, swollen centre of her and located the most sensitive place of all. And from that point on Ellie was lost, without hope of reclaim, stormed by endless exquisite sensations that just as quickly became a kind of sustained torture.

'You are so tight,' Dio muttered in a sensual groan of appreciation.

The ache of need he aroused was unbearable. Ellie writhed out of control, tormented gasps wrenched from her as she clutched at any part of him she could reach. 'Dio, *please*...' she moaned in desperate appeal.

He slid over her, rearranging her with urgent hands. She clashed with blazing eyes and exulted in her femininity, sensing his control was as ragged as her own was non-existent. Fierce hunger seethed in her shamelessly at that instant. She would have walked through fire to lie under him. And then he plunged into her, and the sharp, wrenching pain of that passionate invasion startled her into crying out in surprise.

Dio stilled. Stunned black eyes looked down into hers. '*Cristos*…you can't be!' he exclaimed.

'Not any more…'

Something primitive flared then in his tense gaze. 'You like shocking me, don't you?'

Ellie was blushing like mad now, maddeningly conscious of the tiny smooth shifts with which he was easing his hungry passage all the way inside her. 'Can't talk now,' she mumbled, wholly intent on this new and fascinating experience.

A ragged laugh was torn from Dio. He kissed the crown of her head and began to demonstrate how much more exciting it could get. Raw, out-of-control need possessed her as thoroughly as he did. She couldn't breathe for the insane race of her heart. The world could have ended, and nothing but the pounding surge of his body into hers would have mattered. The intensity of the pleasure drove her wild, and finally off the edge into a hot, wrenching paroxysm of shattering release.

'You should have told me I'd be the first, *pethi mou*,' Dio rasped, out of breath.

'Didn't seem important,' Ellie muttered evasively, revelling in the way he was holding her close to his hot, damp magnificent length, tears of reaction in her softened eyes which she was glad he couldn't see.

Was it possible to fall in love in the space of twenty-four hours? she wondered dreamily, struggling to recognise the person she now felt inside herself, but too happy and fulfilled to feel threatened by that change. *Special?* How special was special? She already knew how special he was to her. She wanted to wrap him up in a big blanket of affection and hug him to death, and Ellie had never felt that soppy in her life before.

'It was important to me,' Dio confided softly. 'Are you hungry?'

'Not really.'

'I can't remember when I last ate,' Dio muttered reflectively.

'Not very sensible,' she told him.

Releasing her, Dio rolled over and reached for the internal phone by the bed to order some food. Then, reaching for her hand, he pulled her out of bed with him. Her arms wrapped round herself as if she was freezing cold, Ellie hovered in the bathroom, watching him switch on the power shower. All of a sudden she felt so horrendously shy. She was being thrown into the deep end of sexual intimacy.

Dio tugged her into the shower with him, either not noticing or deliberately ignoring her discomfiture. 'You really are tiny,' he sighed.

She could feel him staring down at her. 'I'm five foot one inch,' she muttered—adding the inch.

'You looked so funny in that coat at the airport… like a little girl dressing up.'

Ellie couldn't think of anything witty to respond with.

'Why have you gone so quiet?' Dio demanded with sudden force.

'I'm not wearing any clothes and I'm not used to holding conversations in a shower.'

A reluctant laugh of appreciation was dredged from Dio. He lifted her up into his arms like a doll, and hooked her arms round his shoulders. Holding her level with him, he stared into her eyes, his own dark and deep and curiously unguarded. 'Are you on the contraceptive pill?'

Ellie frowned and reddened, wondering why he was asking such a question when she knew that he himself had protected her. 'No…'

'I didn't think you would be. The condom broke,' Dio admitted with unflinching exactitude.

'No…' The warm colour drained from Ellie's

complexion as the implications of that admission sank in. Cold fear snaked through her.

'If anything happens—which I think unlikely—we'll deal with it together.' Dio's breath fanned her parted lips and he slowly, gently kissed her again with incredible expertise.

Snatched in the nick of time from the pessimistic image of having her life ruined by an unplanned pregnancy, as her mother had, Ellie clung to his clearly more optimistic outlook and hurriedly pushed the matter out of her mind. Reality for her had evaporated well over an hour ago, and she was in no hurry for it to intrude again.

'I have plans for you,' Dio shared teasingly between drugging kisses that made Ellie tremble. 'You're going to enjoy being with me.'

They picnicked on the bed. They ate deep-fried courgette, followed by lobster and a Greek salad. Ellie had never eaten lobster in her life, and just about died when she saw it on her plate. She kept on sipping her wine until Dio got around to *his*, and then copied what he did with it. Her own ignorance embarrassed her, reminded her of what vastly different worlds they inhabited, and that was not something she could bear to be reminded of.

'Thank you for what you said on the beach earlier,' Dio murmured levelly. 'It helped me to put the situation into perspective. If either I or my father had once suspected that he had so little time left we would have been instantly reconciled. The biggest irony is that I was already working in that direction.'

'How?' she prompted.

'That conversation you overheard,' Dio reminded her wryly. 'That company I plan to buy out in a few hours' time. My father lost it a long time ago. The reacquisition was to have been a subtle olive branch.'

'Oh, Dio,' Ellie sighed in sympathy. 'So that's why it was so important to you.'

'I'll toast his memory instead. He was a strong, vital man who lived life to the full. He would not want me to remember him with sadness.'

'Explain to me the significance of what I overheard in that office,' Ellie invited, to drive away the vulnerable darkness in his eyes and distract him.

'Let's say we have company A and company B,' Dio responded. 'You buy company A stock, and start a rumour that you're interested in acquiring it. The stock price rises. You resell that stock at a major profit. Then, without warning, you pounce on company B, where the stock price has not risen, and you stage a company buy-out at a good price.'

Ellie shook her head. 'Pretty devious.'

Dio was anything but insulted by that assessment. 'I have that reputation in business. If word of my true intentions were to escape, the stock price of company B would rocket and I wouldn't buy.'

Innately tidy, Ellie couldn't relax until she had removed all the dishes from round the bed. When she returned to the bedroom, Dio had fallen asleep. Her heart, which felt as soft as melted caramel, lurched all over again at the sight of him. He looked exhausted, but rather more at peace than he had looked at the outset of the day when she had woken him up on board the jet. Just for once in her life she was going to go with the flow, she told herself. As a rule she was very, very cautious, preferring to see everything etched in clear black and white before she risked herself. But it was too late for that *now…*

Ellie didn't open her eyes until eight the following morning. Dio was still sound asleep. He even looked gorgeous asleep, she decided, rather glad he wasn't awake, because she was sure she herself looked a mess. But Dio was a long, lithe version of sheer masculine perfection. Even his bronzed skin glowed against the pale bedding.

She crept out of bed, feeling considerably less brave than she had the night before. The intimate ache of her body rather embarrassed her. In the clear light of a beautiful Greek morning Ellie was painfully aware that she had taken a plunge from which there was no turning back. Her emotions were involved up to the hilt, and the level of her absorption in Dio felt frankly scary.

When she put on the candy-pink shorts outfit, she was amused to discover that it wasn't one bit undersized on her. But then she didn't have four-foot-long legs like the store mannequin. She poured herself a glass of iced water from the fridge and pinched an orange and an apple from the bowl on the dining table. In need of fresh air and some temporary physical distance from the male in the bedroom, she went for a walk along the beach.

There was definitely something reassuring about a guy who mentioned having plans for you right from the word go, Ellie told herself urgently, stamping down hard on her anxious misgivings. Dio seemed so honest and open. All right, so she wasn't happy that she had fallen into his bed so quickly, but she was glad that he had been her first lover. At least Dio couldn't get the idea that she made a habit of that sort of thing.

Furthermore, it was a sort of inverted snobbery to imagine that she couldn't possibly have a relationship with Dio just because she was a part-time cleaner in his wretched monolith of a building, wasn't it? It didn't seem to bother him, did it? And she managed the bookshop for Mr Barry. She had a responsible position even if she didn't earn very much. She decided that as soon as she got home she would approach the bank about a loan to buy the bookshop. Only fear of refusal had made her hang back so long.

When she checked her watch, she was surprised to realise that she had been out for a couple of hours. She walked back towards the beach house. From a distance, she saw Dio poised on the verandah, apparently waiting for her. Her mouth ran dry. The closer she got, the more she drank him in. He looked sensational. The unstructured beige jacket he wore over a black tee shirt simply shrieked cool designer elegance. Tailored black chinos hugged his long, powerful thighs. She wished he wasn't wearing sunglasses which masked his eyes.

'I got a call on my mobile,' Dio drawled when she was still several feet away.

And, that quickly, Ellie realised that something was badly wrong. His tone was ice-cold, and so empty of emotion it ran a real chill down her spine.

She came to a halt, green eyes betraying her anxious uncertainty. 'What's wrong?' she asked tautly.

'The minute the market opened, the price of stock in Palco Technic started heading for outer space,' Dio informed her with lethal quietness.

Ellie stared back at him in bewilderment, too shaken by the change in him to immediately understand what he was telling her.

'You said you didn't manage to make that phone call from the airport. But evidently you *did*,' Dio continued with the same lack of emotion. 'You passed on that confidential information you overheard and naturally it's been used. I hope the tip-off paid handsome dividends.'

Ellie unfroze and started forward. 'The *only* call I made from the airport was made on your phone! For goodness' sake, Dio…' she protested feelingly. 'If something's gone wrong, it's got nothing to do with me. I haven't passed on any information…I wouldn't even know where to pass it *to*!'

'One too many coincidences, Ellie. Like where were you when I woke up this morning?'

She blinked in disconcertion. 'I—'

'Tell me, were you afraid of how I might react when the bad news broke and the balloon went up?' Dio enquired flatly. 'You knew that I'd find out what you'd done before you got off this island, but you were too greedy to stop and think about that, weren't you?'

The sun was beating down on Ellie. Perspiration was dampening her skin. But inside herself the coldness of shock was spreading like a glacier. Now that she had finally grasped what she was being accused of—selling the content of that wretched conversation in some covert phone call— if anything, she felt even more bemused.

'Dio, you've got this all wrong,' Ellie protested. 'If that information has got out somehow, I'm sorry, but I don't like being accused of something I didn't do. I did warn you that there was someone else listening at that doorway—'

Savage derision curled Dio's expressive mouth. 'Don't insult my intelligence—'

'What intelligence?' Ellie demanded thinly, an unstable combination of anger and piercing fear beginning to rise out of her shock. 'If you had any, it *should* be telling you that it's highly unlikely to be me responsible for any information leak!'

'You blew my deal. And then you crawled into

bed with me and practically prostituted yourself in the hope of placating me,' Dio spelt out with menacing softness.

That savage judgement hung there in the hot, still air. Ellie shivered, white as death, her beautiful face a frozen oval.

Dio whipped off his sunglasses and surveyed her with eyes that glittered black as night over her. 'No…looking at you now, I *do* believe it was a little more personal than that,' he drawled with silken insolence, his accent licking around every vowel sound in the stillness.

'You bastard,' Ellie whispered, reacting to that calculated cruelty with instinctive recoil.

'So I went slumming for one night,' Dio derided. 'It was an experience, but not one I ever intend to repeat.'

Ellie threw back her bright head, eyes burning like emerald daggers. 'No, *I* was the one slumming, Dio. All you've got is a bottomless bank account. You have as much class as an illiterate goat-herd!'

Dio jerked and froze to the spot. Ellie stalked up onto the verandah, brushing past him to gain entry to the beach house. All that was guiding her was a somewhat formless desire to get some shoes on and escape. She sped into the bedroom, where her clothing was.

As she crossed the threshold, a powerful hand suddenly closed round her forearm. 'Say that again,' Dio invited in a raw undertone of pure menace.

'You have as much class as an illiterate goat-herd,' Ellie framed woodenly, staring blindly into space. 'And, in making that comparison, I have no doubt that I am insulting the goat-herd. He might well be poor and decent, and if he's poor and mean, well, at least he's got some excuse—'

'Whereas I?' Dio slotted in, a whole octave louder in volume.

Ellie's heart was hammering like a storm warning. She could feel his rage like a hurricane, churning up the atmosphere, but she couldn't suppress her overwhelming need to hit back. 'You are rich and privileged and pig-ignorant. Now get your hands off me!'

A split second later, her feet left the marble floor and a strangled screech escaped her. Dio brought her down on the bed in a startlingly fast landing that left her breathless and pinned her there. He was ashen pale beneath his bronzed skin, dark, deep-set eyes now a blaze of flashing gold intimidation. 'If you were a man, I'd kill you for such insults!'

'You're f-frightening me...' Ellie mumbled truthfully.

An expression of extreme distaste flashed across Dio's darkly handsome features. He straightened up and backed off instantaneously. 'The helicopter's waiting up at the villa for you,' he delivered between clenched teeth, with openly challenged restraint. 'Pack and get out! Don't set foot in the Alexiakis International building again.

Pale as the pristine white sheet spread beneath her, Ellie swung her legs off the side of the bed and sat there. 'I thought I could love you, and now I hate you,' she muttered sickly.

With a contemptuous gesture of one lean brown hand, Dio sent a handful of banknotes fluttering down onto the soft deep carpet at her feet.

Ellie stared speechless at all those fifty pound notes.

'As you said, business comes first and last in your life. If it's any consolation, you gave me a great night.'

Ellie's innate survival skills rose above the devastating sense of betrayal that momentarily threatened to overwhelm her. 'Is this my plane fare home from Athens?'

'*Cristos*...what's that supposed to mean?' Dio raked at her.

'That little people like me have to think of practical stuff like that. I don't know how much a flight home would cost,' she extended doggedly, refusing to look at him, refusing to let herself *feel* anything at all.

'You collect your ticket at the terminal.'

'Then all I need is transport home once I get back to London.' Ellie picked up one note, resolving to send him the change, and then she stiffened. 'What about Meg?'

'The other cleaner? What do you think?'

'That if you sack Meg too, you will live to regret it.' Slowly, very slowly, Ellie raised her head, eyes as cold as his own now as she made the worst threat she could imagine. 'I'll go to the newspapers, Dio. Since they seem so interested in you, I'll give them chapter and verse on this whole sleazy little episode and then compensate Meg with the proceeds...'

Dio studied her with a quality of incredulous disgust that was unmistakable. Inwardly, Ellie cringed from that look and, terrified of betraying any further weakness, she got up on cotton wool legs. Turning her back to him, she tipped her old canvas shoes out of the relevant carrier bag and slid her feet into them. With a nerveless grip on the bag that contained the rest of what she had been wearing that first evening, she walked past him, her head as high as she could hold it.

It seemed to take for ever to reach the lift in the villa, for ever to walk the length of that opulent endless hall, shoulders and spine aching with the rigidity of unnatural control. The helicopter was parked on the heli-pad a hundred yards from the entrance. She climbed in and closed her eyes tight, shallowly breathing in and out, struggling to maintain control and, most of all, not to actually *think* about what she had foolishly brought on herself.

But the first stab of self-loathing still escaped and pierced deep long before she reached Athens. Ellie wasn't used to making mistakes. In fact, Ellie was very cautious, particularly with men. So when the events of the previous thirty-six hours flashed before her, she could not begin to credit her own foolish wanton behaviour. Before long she decided that she had got exactly what she deserved. She had invited all that pain and humiliation.

When had she contrived to forget that she was

with the same modest guy who had announced earlier in the day that he could 'persuade' her to belong to him? She shivered beneath the sting of that memory. It was even more of a hard lesson to acknowledge that she had actually felt *close* to a male capable of misjudging her to such an extent. He hadn't even listened to her attempt to defend herself.

What did she want with somebody that stupid and prejudiced anyway? The trouble was, nothing had ever hurt Ellie so much in five long years...

CHAPTER FIVE

ELLIE rearranged the book display in the window for the second time that day.

'Cup of tea, Ellie?' Horace Barry suggested.

It was a lashing wet day and there wasn't a customer in the shop. Ellie focused on her elderly employer, the kindly concern visible in his lined features, and forced a strained smile. 'Lovely... thanks.'

Grateful that the older man would never dream of asking prying questions, Ellie stood behind the counter sipping her tea and watching the rain stream down the window and the door. She had been back home for two days, but what had happened on the island of Chindos haunted her more with every passing hour. How could she have been such an idiot?

Sex was a dangerous fire to play with; she had always known that. She had always believed that physical intimacy belonged in stable relationships. It was humiliating to accept that she had recklessly gone to bed with a man she had known for little more than a day. She had had a choice and, relying on feelings rather than intelligence, she had made the wrong choice. She should have kept Dio Alexiakis at arm's length. And if that little accident with contraception which Dio had mentioned with such supreme cool had consequences, she would have nobody to blame but herself, she reflected fearfully.

Mr Barry went home early. Just before closing time, a delivery man arrived with a large bouquet. 'Miss Eleanor Morgan?'

'I don't think I'm the Eleanor Morgan you're looking for,' Ellie told him drily, never having received flowers in her life, and certainly not an enormous bunch of costly white roses.

'This is the address.'

Her heart beating very fast as she thought of the only person she knew who could afford such a gesture, Ellie signed for the bouquet and tore the accompanying card out of the envelope. Three words. 'From the goat-herd.'

Ellie turned white, and then furious pink. She tore the card into pieces as small as confetti and tossed them in the bin below the counter.

Evidently the roses were Dio's idea of an apology.

Her soft full mouth compressed. Had he somehow established that she wasn't the source of the information leak? Someone else must have rammed that reality down his arrogant throat, Ellie decided bleakly. Certainly Dio himself hadn't cherished the slightest doubt of her guilt. No, Dio had had no trouble whatsoever believing that the sneaky little cleaner had lied to him, deceived him and finally betrayed his precious plans. She hoped he's lost a mint of money on the deal going wrong. He deserved to.

The phone rang. She answered it.

'I'd like to speak to Ellie…'

Ellie froze at the startling familiarity of Dio's rich, dark drawl.

Silence filled with static buzzed on the line.

'What do you want?' she enquired curtly.

'I'll be back in London by nine this evening. I want to see you.'

'Nothing doing,' Ellie said after a truly staggered pause in which to absorb that smooth announcement of intent.

'Ellie…' Dio breathed, and the way he said her name made her clench the phone so tight that her fingers ached.

'Is Meg still employed?' she demanded brittly.

'Yes.'

'Fine...' Ellie released her pent-up breath in a jerky exhalation of relief. 'I presume that means that I can have my job back too?'

'We'll discuss that later—'

'Dio, we are never going to meet again in this lifetime,' Ellie asserted, her temper steadily climbing. 'All I've got to say to you I can say now. You *owe* me my job back!'

'I can find you alternative employment—'

'Look, what's it to you if I'm working on level eight?' Ellie raked down the line at him with furious resentment. 'You think I'm going to gossip about you with the women I work with? You've just got to be joking! Electric shock treatment wouldn't drag a confession from me!'

'We'll talk about it this evening.'

'I'm not seeing you again. I don't *want* to see you again! You're trying to bully me and I'm not having it. If you don't let me go back to work, I'll go to an employment tribunal with a complaint of unfair dismissal. I know my rights, Dio.'

'Ellie, you just said that electric shock treatment wouldn't drag a confession from you,' Dio reminded her in a maddeningly lazy drawl. 'It wouldn't work to be that sensitive with a tribunal.'

'Surely you don't believe I'd tell the whole truth? A convincingly *sneaky* little liar like me?' Ellie hissed in a sizzling undertone. 'Naturally, I'd lie!'

The silence full of static returned.

'If you want to return to work next week, I won't stand in your way.' Dio ground out that concession with audible exasperation.

'I'm going in tonight. Just forget we ever collided, Dio. *I* certainly have,' Ellie told him, and slammed down the phone.

Did he think she was prepared to see him just to hear some explanation about who had really blabbed about his confidential plans? Did he really think she was interested? Did he fondly imagine an apology was likely to change anything? Were all rich men that arrogant? Fizzing with turbulent emotion, Ellie locked up the shop and mounted the stairs to her bedsit behind the storeroom on the first floor.

The very last thing she needed was to *see* Dio Alexiakis again. Who would wish to be faced with the reminder of their lowest moment? Throwing together a sandwich with trembling hands, Ellie took two bites of it and then dumped it. Twenty minutes later, she set out for work at the Alexiakis International building. Why couldn't he just leave her alone? Couldn't he appreciate that he was just embarrassing and annoying her?

When Ellie walked into the building, the big portrait of Dio in the ground-floor foyer really offended her. On canvas, Dio just emanated cool, sophisticated charm. Fresh flowers always adorned the side table below the painting. It looked remarkably like a shrine to her embittered and unimpressed gaze.

The supervisor, a thin, sour woman, frowned when Ellie signed in. 'You took off on Monday night without a word to anyone,' she censured. 'You didn't even phone in sick. I had to put in a report to Personnel.'

'Yes. I expect you did. I'm sorry.' Ellie added another pound of flesh to Dio's mounting tally of sins and fumed all the way up to level eight.

Midway through her shift, she went down to the basement restroom for her usual cup of coffee. Meg dropped into the vacant seat beside her. 'Where on earth did you go on Monday evening?' she demanded. 'I was so worried when you didn't come down for your break. I was scared there'd been a row, because that bloke you told me about—'

'What bloke?'

'You know, the one that was annoying you.' Meg

frowned at her. 'Big blond bloke called Bolton. He walked right up to me the minute I began work on your floor and demanded to know where you were.'

Ellie paled. 'Sorry.'

'I *had* to tell him, love. Did he come upstairs looking for you?'

Ellie stilled. 'I don't know…I didn't see him,' she muttered, suddenly wondering if it was Ricky Bolton who had overheard Dio's wretched profiteering plans.

The conversation of two other women nearby attracted her attention.

'I bet she's just a secretary or something…'

'Not the way she was done up, with the hat and all,' the other argued vehemently. 'Anyway, why would he take a secretary to his dad's funeral?'

Ellie cleared her dry throat. 'Who are they talking about?'

'The mystery blonde Mr Alexiakis arrived in Athens with. A secretary!' Meg chuckled. 'Not in *those* clothes!'

'Some secretaries are very highly qualified and earn top salaries,' Ellie hastened to point out.

One of the other women leant across the gap separating them and said, 'That blonde piece was a dead ringer for you, Ellie.' She gave an outrageous wink. 'And you did go AWOL that night. Anything you'd like to confess?'

'Me...*me*?' Ellie repeated, sharply disconcerted and striving for more convincing vigour.

'Ellie would be too busy lecturing our Dio about sexism in the workplace to get off with him!' someone else mocked.

'I'm rather behind tonight. I'd better get back to work,' Ellie told Meg breathlessly as the dialogue roamed away from her again, leaving her limp.

She caught the bus home at the end of her shift, feeling both tired and stressed out. As she walked down the street where she lived, she could not help but notice the long silver limousine parked outside the shop. Fierce tension tautened her slim figure and her heart raced so fast it was a challenge to breathe. As she approached, Dio Alexiakis got out of the car, the movement fluid and controlled, without any suggestion of haste.

As usual, he looked spectacular. Charcoal-grey suit, crisp shadow stripe shirt, elegant silk tie in muted shades. Ellie's heart went from racing to sinking. Dio looked every inch what he was, she acknowledged dully. A very rich and powerful businessman, highly sophisticated and exquisitely well groomed. How she had *ever* for one second imagined that she could have a relationship with someone like him?

Ellie removed her keys from her bag with an unsteady hand. 'You're not playing fair, Dio. I told you I didn't want this,' she reminded him.

'I hurt you and I'm sorry,' Dio murmured steadily.

Unprepared for a blunt assertion of that ego-battering truth, Ellie twisted her head away. Her strained eyes stung with tears as she fumbled blindly to get the key into the lock and get the shop door safely shut behind her again.

Dio plucked the key from her nerveless grip, opened the door and stood back.

Ellie stepped inside and adjusted the alarm so that it wouldn't go off. 'I just don't want to speak to you...OK?' she said stiltedly.

'No. It's not OK. I want to talk to you.'

Ellie swallowed hard. All he probably wanted to do was explain and go away again. With as much dignity as she could muster, she simply shrugged as if she didn't really care either way. Dio followed her up the steep narrow staircase behind the counter. She unlocked the door of her bedsit and switched on the lamp by her bed.

It was a spacious room and she was proud of it. She had painted the walls a sunny yellow, put up posters, and covered the armchair with a colourful throw. Tossing her keys on the gate-leg table by the window, she turned back to him with pronounced reluctance.

Dio studied her with an intensity she could feel right through to her bones. She flushed and folded her arms, suddenly horribly conscious of her serviceable rain jacket, faded jeans and sweater. In the act of tilting her chin, she connected with glittering black eyes. She quivered, treacherous heat pooling between her thighs, a strength of craving that appalled her instantly awakened.

'Come home with me' Dio demanded thickly.

'No!' Ellie gasped, reeling in bemusement from that invitation.

Dark colour scored his hard cheekbones. His dense lashes swept down low over his stunning gaze and he breathed in deep, his tension as strong as her own. 'You're right. We have to talk this out first,' he conceded with gritty reluctance.

First? Ellie spun away on legs that trembled, shattered that he could reduce her to such a level with just one smouldering glance.

'I went off on a tangent with you on the island,'

Dio admitted without hesitation. 'When my chief accountant called me with the bad news, I cut him short. I didn't want to discuss it any further. I'm afraid I just assumed that you had made that phone call from the airport. I was outraged.'

'Yes,' Ellie conceded stiffly.

'But this morning I learnt that you had been telling the truth all along. There *was* someone else there that night. His arrival and his departure were recorded by the security camera in the corridor,' Dio revealed ruefully. 'If I had been in a more focused frame of mind at the time, I would've recalled the presence of that camera and I would have been able to check out your story immediately.'

Ellie nodded in silence without looking back at him, her delicate profile taut.

'I have a hot temper. But I don't usually rush into making instant judgements on the basis of circumstantial evidence,' Dio continued.

'Well, it didn't look good for me, did it?' Ellie responded with determined lightness, keen to bring his visit to a speedy conclusion. 'You didn't know me, so how could you know that I wouldn't do something like that?'

'You're being very generous, but that's not an excuse I need to hide behind. We had spent enough time together. I *should* have known,' Dio contradicted levelly. 'I very much regret the way I treated you on Chindos. I was…brutal.'

Ellie didn't argue that point. She stared at her own feet, eager to focus on anything that helped her to resist the temptation to look at him again. He was making resistance difficult. He hadn't leapt on the excuse she had offered him, as most men would have done. He wasn't trying to lessen his own offence. He wasn't trying to deny that he had cruelly humiliated her.

The silence stretched and stretched. She knew he was waiting for her to say something, but she had nothing to say.

Dio exhaled in a soft hiss. 'The employee who tipped off one of my competitors was an accounts manager called—'

'Ricky Bolton?' Ellie interrupted before she could think better of it.

His dark eyes narrowed. 'How did you know who it was? I thought you didn't see the man.'

'I didn't, but during my break this evening Meg told me that he'd asked where I was that night, and he is an accounts manager—'

'Why would Bolton have been asking where you were?'

Ellie grimaced. 'He was the guy who was always trying to chat me up on level eight.'

At that admission, Dio's jawline took on an aggressive slant. 'I was even denied the pleasure of sacking him. He resigned from his job the next day. He exchanged the information he had picked up for a more senior position in the other company—not that he'll be there for long.'

'Why not?'

A grim smile curved Dio's wide, sensual mouth. 'He has no company loyalty. How can he be trusted? The first excuse they get, he'll be fired.'

'Oh…' Her shadowed gaze clung to that lean strong face, her mouth running dry, her breath feathering in her throat. 'You don't seem as angry as I thought you'd still be.'

'I put my plans for a buy-out on hold. And before word got out I made a healthy profit selling the stock I held in company A…' His brilliant dark eyes held hers as he utilised the same terminology he had employed to explain his tactics as they had lain in bed together at the beach house.

Ellie flushed, but she still couldn't break that enervating visual link.

'As for company B, my competitors mistakenly assumed that if *I* was interested, company B must have some wonderful new technology under wraps. They bought a massive amount of their stock,' Dio continued with a sardonic edge to his deep-pitched drawl. 'Having now discovered otherwise, when they unload that stock, they are likely to make a loss.'

'So in the end you'll probably pick up that company for a song...'

Silence fell and lingered. Dio studied her with dark, deep, intent eyes. Ellie tensed like a mouse sensing a cat. She was unbearably aware of his potent masculinity. Indeed, beneath that slumbrous appraisal her breasts stirred and ached, their sensitive peaks straining to wanton tautness. Hot pink embellished her cheekbones.

In one fluid movement, Dio closed the distance between them. 'I won't hurt you like that again, Ellie.'

The colour in her face receded. 'I think you should leave now, Dio.'

His winged ebony brows pleated, his surprise unconcealed. 'Why?'

And with that one word, which revealed just how easily Dio had expected to win her forgiveness,

Ellie was armoured against him. All weakness put back under safe lock and key. 'Surely that's obvious?' she murmured drily. 'What happened on the island isn't ever going to happen again. We've got nothing more to say to each other.'

'I won't let you go,' Dio declared in a silken tone of steel.

Her green eyes flared bright with resentment. 'Who the heck do you think you are to say that to me?'

'Your lover,' Dio responded softly.

Ellie paled at that retaliation.

'I told you I wasn't into one-night stands,' he reminded her steadily. 'You're still angry with me, Ellie. I understand that, but it's hardly an insurmountable problem.'

'Whether I'm angry or not is irrelevant,' Ellie protested tautly. 'On the island...*us*...well, it was more like a fantasy, a dream.'

Dio dealt her a sizzling smile. 'Thanks.'

Ellie stiffened, annoyed that he wasn't taking her seriously. 'But now we're back in the real world, Dio.'

'Even on Chindos, I was not aware that we had left it—'

'Well, I *certainly* had,' Ellie countered vehemently. 'It was my natural environment. Idyllic moonlit beach, handsome foreigner saying all the right things…and pow, suddenly we're in bed!'

Dio frowned. 'What are you trying to say?'

'We let ourselves forget who we both are,' Ellie stated curtly.

'And what are we but two people who desire each other?' Dio demanded forcefully.

'I'm an ordinary working girl and you're a super-rich Greek tycoon! Stop trying to duck the issue,' Ellie told him in exasperation. 'I could have been the cleaner on the top floor all my life and you'd never have noticed that I was even alive!'

'I would have noticed you—'

'No, you *wouldn't* have!' Ellie was determined to drive her point home. 'Because someone like you doesn't really ever look at someone like me—'

'But now that I have looked, I'm not backing off,' Dio interrupted with stubborn assurance. 'As for you being an ordinary working girl, that's a problem I would be happy to deal with.'

'A problem?' Ellie gave him a bemused look. 'What are you talking about?'

'I want to keep the fantasy going. Fantasy I understand,' Dio confessed as he calmly linked his arms round her small but taut figure. 'I think you're adorable, *yineka mou.*'

'A-adorable…' Ellie echoed weakly, feeling like a woman trying to stem a damburst with a piece of paper.

'There's no need for you to work,' Dio murmured with a husky intimacy that sent a flick of fire dancing over her entire skin surface. 'I'll buy you an apartment—'

'An a-apartment?' Ellie stammered in total bewilderment.

Dio ran a long brown forefinger in a silken caress along her sensitive jawbone and tipped up her chin to gaze hungrily down into her widening eyes. 'I'm Greek. I want to take care of you in every way. You look stunned. Why? I told you on Chindos that I had plans for you.'

In serious shock, Ellie parted her lips, but no sound came out the first time. Her vocal cords had seized up. The second time, a thready version of her usual brisk voice emerged. 'Let me get this straight…*you* are asking *me* to be your mistress?'

'I am asking you to be my woman,' Dio countered with megawatt cool.

'Your little toy…' Ellie squeezed out, since her lungs felt as if they were on the brink of collapse.

Oh, what a bitter irony that he should make such a suggestion! She didn't know whether to laugh or scream.

Dio studied her with a reproachful light in his dark gaze. 'That is not how it would be between us.'

'Would you ask a woman from your own background to be your mistress?' Ellie could not resist demanding.

Dio flung back his arrogant dark head, black eyes glittering with stars. 'You are the only woman I have ever asked.'

'Sorry, I'm not available,' Ellie told him without a single shade of regret.

Dio slid lean brown fingers into the fall of her silvery hair, holding her imprisoned. Scorching eyes roamed over her flushed and angry face. 'You're hooked. You just won't admit it yet. You want me as much as I want you—'

'Right now, I could give you freezer burn!' Ellie warned him.

'Let's see…shall we?'

'Dio, *no*—'

But Dio crushed her soft mouth under his. And then he sent his tongue delving with carnal expertise into the tender interior of her mouth. Plunging and withdrawing, he set fire to her every skin cell in a charged and erotic reminder of how he had once invaded her quivering and eager body. Her thighs trembled. Helpless in the grip of that excitement, she pushed into the lean, hard heat and muscularity of his powerful frame. Recognising the bold thrust of his erection against her, she melted into hot liquid honey inside herself.

With a shuddering groan, Dio cupped two big hands round her face and stared down at her with raw sexual hunger. 'Why shouldn't I offer you financial support? It would be as much for my own convenience as yours. I want you to travel with me. I want you to *be* there for me…'

The fevered heat in Ellie's bloodstream drained away, axed by his physical withdrawal of passion but even more by his candour. 'What you want is a sex slave on tap…'

'I'd be bored rigid with a sex slave,' Dio retorted with unblemished cool.

A ragged and involuntary laugh escaped Ellie. But, raising her hands, she firmly detached herself from him and stepped back. 'You are *so* smooth, Dio. And this ridiculous conversation is totally pointless. You're wasting your time.'

His dark, deep-set eyes rested on her, his strong bone structure clenching. 'You belong with me—'

'No, I definitely don't.' Ellie tossed back her head as she challenged that contention. 'Nor do I have the slightest desire to be kept by anyone. The hours I work, I haven't even got room for a man in my life. I should be furious with you for asking me to be your mistress. But you *did* remind me that you are Greek. I suppose I have to make allowances for cultural differences...'

A dark rise of blood now marked Dio's spectacular cheekbones. 'I think you want me to chase you—'

'That's your ego talking. What I *want* is to forget we ever met,' Ellie contradicted with fierce conviction, her fingernails biting into her palms. 'But you're so used to being top of every woman's wish list that when I say no you can't accept that I *mean* no!'

Black eyes burned into hers in ferocious challenge. 'If I walk away now, it's over.'

At that warning, and in spite of all she had said, Ellie's breath snarled up in her throat. She felt hollow in the taut, waiting silence which followed.

Without another word, Dio strode to the door. And then he was gone.

Ellie waited for a few minutes, and then went downstairs to lock up after him. When she came back up, the room felt empty and cold. It was as if Dio had taken all the light and energy with him. She dismissed that fanciful impression and strove without success to appreciate the irony of the proposition he had laid before her. After all, no persuasion known to mankind would have persuaded Ellie to even *consider* such a lifestyle...

Her mother had been her father's mistress for sixteen years, a covert relationship full of lies and endless pretences. From the day she was old enough to finally understand why her mother had no friends in the small coastal town where they had lived, Ellie had been bitterly ashamed of her parentage. Leigh Morgan had decided that she could not live without the married father of her child, and in so doing, she had wrecked her own life.

Ellie suppressed her memories of her less than idyllic childhood and grimaced. No, she would never be guilty of repeating her mother's mistakes. In a couple of weeks Dio probably wouldn't even remember her name. Unfortunately, she suspected that she was going to be remembering him for a very long time...

Slicing through her defences, Dio had sent her flying high into the realms of romantic fantasy. He had taken her to paradise in bed. But within hours he had mercifully brought her back down to earth with a jarring crash. He had hurt her more than she had known she could be hurt. She had learnt that she was far more naive than she would ever have been prepared to admit.

Not a bad lesson to learn, Ellie told herself, striving to feel more upbeat. The excitement was over now. She had resisted Dio Alexiakis. She had done the right thing. But why hadn't she appreciated how dreadful doing the right thing might make her feel?

CHAPTER SIX

MIDWAY through the following week, Ellie told Mr Barry that she had finally made an appointment at the bank.

'Why?'

Ellie smiled, thinking that her elderly employer was becoming very absent-minded. 'So that I can apply for a loan to buy this business,' she reminded him gently.

Horace Barry looked dismayed. 'Leave that for a while yet, Ellie,' he urged.

Bewildered by that reaction, Ellie murmured reluctantly, 'I suppose I *could* cancel the appointment—'

'Yes...yes, much the best thing for now,' he cut in to agree with a pronounced air of relief.

With a muttered reference to some books that required sorting, the older man then took himself off without offering any further explanation. Ellie frowned. Wasn't he quite as eager to retire as he had always said he was? What else could it be?

Keen to save on estate agency fees, Horace Barry had given her to understand that if she was able to offer a fair price by the end of the year, the shop was hers. Ellie told herself not to make mountains out of molehills. It wouldn't hurt her to wait, but she was disappointed. Just then, the challenge of taking on her own business would have been very welcome.

Another two weeks passed by on leaden feet for Ellie. Mr Barry was a quiet man, but he had become exceptionally quiet. Almost evasive with her. Troubled and distracted by that suspicion, Ellie had to glance at the calendar in her room one evening before she belatedly noticed the absence of a certain telling pen-mark. All of a sudden Ellie saw that she had something far more immediate to worry about.

Stress and sleepless nights had probably disrupted her monthly cycle, she told herself in dismay. She was only about a week late. But the more she worried about the possibility of being pregnant, the more likely a development it seemed. She might well have conceived. She was young and healthy and, according to her calculations, the timing of that contraceptive failure could not have been worse.

As Ellie entered the Alexiakis International building for work that same evening, she saw Dio for the first time in almost three weeks. Tall, blue-black hair gleaming under the lights, his bold, bronzed profile commanding, he was striding towards the executive lift, three other men in his wake. Shock made Ellie's stomach flip right over. She came to an involuntary halt on legs that felt distinctly wobbly. Her head swam and she gulped in oxygen, feeling perspiration break out on her skin.

'How are you, Ellie?' a deep, dark drawl enquired with leaden casualness.

Blinking furiously, Ellie focused on a pair of polished hand-stitched leather shoes and slowly lifted her head. Her wide, incredulous gaze centred on Dio and stayed there, locked onto him like a guided missile, her heart pounding like crazy. Black fathomless eyes stared down into hers.

'You look like a ghost facing an exorcist,' Dio murmured in flat continuation, looking her over with unashamed and even more inappropriate thoroughness.

Noticing his three former companions holding the lift for his benefit while watching the encounter with the equivalent of dropped jaws, Ellie forced her brain to spring back into gear. 'Go away, for goodness' sake!' she urged, her colour high. 'You're not supposed to know me!'

'Damned if I do and damned if I don't,' Dio rhymed with sardonic amusement. 'Why are women so irrational?'

'Why are men so unbelievably thick?' Ellie breathed, sidestepping him to hurry on past with a downbent head. Before she had completed that escape, however, she noticed a couple of the other cleaners nearby. Their attention was welded to her with speculative heat. Ellie's heart sank.

When she went down for her break later, she was intensely uncomfortable. If one of her co-workers had challenged her openly about her encounter with Dio, she would have known that nothing suspicious had been detected. But the sudden silence which greeted her appearance, the covert glances and the buzz that broke out when she left again told her otherwise. And what other reaction could she have expected? she asked herself sickly.

Dio hadn't just given her a fleeting nod or a passing word. In the act of stepping into the lift, Dio had come all the way back across the foyer to acknowledge her and embark on a conversation. What on earth had possessed him? Didn't he appreciate how much he had exposed her to adverse comment?

Meg Bucknall followed her into the service lift. 'I thought I'd better wait and have a word with you in private,' she admitted frankly.

Ellie tried not to stiffen and nodded.

'Ellie, the girls were adding two and two and making four before you even started your shift,' Meg shared ruefully. 'Everyone knows you switched with me that night and then just vanished for most of that week.'

'I didn't think anyone would be that interested.'

'In the normal way of it, they wouldn't have been. But a few of them had already joked about how much you looked like that blonde with Mr Alexiakis in Greece. None of them were suspicious…but him going out of his way to speak to you tonight was strange enough to confirm the wildest rumours.'

Ellie had too much respect for the older woman to embark on frantic denials. On her first night back to work she had known that Meg was disconcerted by her failure to offer an explanation of her disappearance. 'I'll ride out the gossip,' she muttered tautly.

The older woman sighed. 'A couple of weeks

ago, Mr Alexiakis walked past me and said, "Goodnight, Mrs Bucknall," for the *first* time ever. I couldn't help but know that something had changed somewhere. I would have sworn he didn't even *know* my name, never mind take note of me being around!'

Ellie coloured as she recalled accusing Dio of not even noticing his more humble employees.

'I've no time for gossip.' Meg's eyes were troubled. 'It's *you* I'm worrying about—'

'I'm fine…sadder but wiser,' Ellie confided tightly as the lift reached her floor.

Meg grimaced. 'I wish I could give that young man a piece of my mind—'

'I'm not a child, Meg.'

'No,' Meg conceded grudgingly as Ellie stepped out. 'But you needn't try to kid me that you're in *his* league either!'

It was no comfort to be reminded of that salient fact. Ellie was already far too well aware of it. One reckless night which could well change the whole course of her life, she reflected with a feeling shiver. Her mother had been a single parent. Ellie knew better than most just how difficult it was to raise a child alone. She was probably being foolishly pessimistic, she told herself. Even so, she decided to buy a kit and do a pregnancy test for herself the following day. It would be a lot quicker than waiting to get an appointment with her doctor.

She was emerging from one of the offices on level eight when the lift next to the reception area pinged. She turned her head, expecting to see the security guard on his round, and froze when she saw Dio Alexiakis striding down the corridor towards her.

This time she noticed every tiny detail of his appearance. He was wearing a superb silver-grey suit, cut to enhance every powerful line of his magnificent physique. Her heartbeat thudded preternaturally slow in her eardrums. His lean, dark features had a slightly keener edge then she recalled; his sensational cheekbones were more defined, the hollows below a little deeper. But even the faint shadows now etched beneath his stunning eyes added an exotic tinge of drama to his spectacular good-looks, she reflected in a sudden surge of bitter anger. She hated the way he made her feel. Breathless and excited, and then foolish and unbearably sad…

Ellie spun away and plugged in the floor-polisher, determined just to get on with her job.

The polisher fired into noisy motion but almost as suddenly lost power.

Ellie whirled round. Having switched off the electric current, Dio straightened, surveying her disconcerted face with brilliant black eyes of challenge. 'Stop running away,' he derided.

Unprepared for that angle of attack, Ellie said tautly, 'I don't know what you're talking about—'

'Yes, you do. You're trying to hide behind the fact that you work for me. But it's too late for that,' Dio told her with sardonic cool.

'I just want you to leave me alone.'

Dio gazed steadily back at her. 'Every time you look at me, you tell me the exact opposite.' He reached down for her hand before she could guess his intention. 'Your pulse is racing. You're trembling—'

'With annoyance!' Ellie tugged her wrist free and spun away again. 'I know what I want out of life and, believe me, you're not part of the package!'

'What features in the package?'

'You really want to know?'

'I really want to know,' Dio confirmed levelly.

'All right. I'm hoping to buy the bookshop. That's why I run two jobs. I've been saving up for a long time and I'll be applying for a loan soon,' she admitted flatly.

'I'll offer you a loan now, on a straight business basis,' Dio informed her lazily.

Ellie groaned out loud in frustration, marched into the next office down the corridor and snatched up the wastepaper bin. 'You just don't get it, do you?' she condemned when she emerged again. 'I don't want any favours. I don't *need* any help.'

'But you're making your employment here a barrier between us.'

'Dio…you wouldn't recognise a solid brick wall as a barrier!' Ellie snapped.

'I shouldn't have asked you to be my mistress,' he murmured sibilantly.

Ellie was tempted into looking at him again, the hard knot of anger inside her loosening ever so slightly. 'No—'

'It was too soon,' Dio completed.

'You are a *really* slow learner!' Ellie delivered with waspish bite.

Vibrant amusement shimmered in his stunning dark eyes. 'I've missed having you around, *pethi mou.*'

That smile warmed her like summer sunshine. She dragged her eyes from him, as if that sudden heat burned her. 'So you're bored with sycophancy and in need of novelty. Have you ever thought of a dating agency?'

'You finish work soon. Let me take you out to eat somewhere.'

Ellie studied him where he lounged up against the door like a sleek, dark predator at rest. He aroused the most terrifyingly powerful hunger in her. She thought of all the nights she had tossed and turned, unable to get him out of her mind and hating herself for being so weak she couldn't control her own thoughts. But there it was, this aching, hurting craving that went way beyond physical desire...

'Ellie...' Dio prompted gently.

'I finish work and go to *bed*, Dio,' she stressed curtly, bending down to plug in the polisher again.

'So we skip the food.'

Anger lancing through her in response to that provocative suggestion, Ellie came upright again very fast. But that sudden movement engulfed her in a wave of dizziness. Her view of Dio and the well-lit corridor lurched, and then blurred out of focus. With a muffled gasp of fright she went down and down into the beckoning darkness, her legs crumpling beneath her.

When Ellie began to recover consciousness, she felt nauseous and dazed. Her lashes lifted slowly. Dio was so close she could see the tiny golden lights in his eyes and every inky individual spike of his lush lashes. They were in a lift and he was carrying her, she finally registered, twin discoveries which confused her even more. 'Dio…'

'What?' he demanded with unconcealed aggression, powerful arms tightening round her to keep her firmly wedged against his hard, muscular chest.

'What happened?' she mumbled heavily.

'You fainted.'

A frown indented her damp brow as she fought to regain her wits. 'I don't faint…'

'I've had it with this cleaning lark,' Dio ground out, his jawline squaring. 'It's obvious that you're not fit for it.'

'Dio…put me down!'

'If I put you down, you'll fall over again! You look terrible, but then that's not very surprising, is it?' Dio continued in the same accusing tone. 'You work six days a week in that bookshop, and more than half the time you're left to cope on your own there.'

'How do you *know* that?' Ellie gasped, taken aback by his knowledge.

'I made it my business to know.' Black eyes gleamed down into hers. 'Your other employer has got it made. He wanders in around lunchtime and heads home again mid-afternoon. How can you expect to work all day and then put in five nights here in a physically demanding job?'

'I'm young, and healthy as a horse,' Ellie protested as the lift doors sprang open, belatedly prompting her to demand to know where on earth he was taking her.

'I'm taking you home.' With long, forceful strides, Dio headed out across the ground-floor foyer towards the line of exit doors.

With difficulty, Ellie dragged her attention from him and took in the presence of the security guards at the main reception area. One of them was rushing to get a door open. The other two were gazing rigidly into space with the fixed expressions of men who had had a really good look at them coming out of the lift but were determined not to betray any reaction that might cause offence.

Belatedly appreciating the spectacle Dio was making of them both, Ellie groaned out loud. 'How am I ever going to work here again after this?'

'Goodnight, Mr Alexiakis,' the guard swinging open the door said stiltedly.

'*Ne*…yes, it *is* a good night,' Dio drawled with a truly staggering lack of self-consciousness.

Ellie just closed her eyes tight, feeling the cool air of outdoors chill her burning cheeks. 'If I didn't still feel so awful, I'd strangle you for this, Dio!'

Unrepentant, Dio stowed her in the back seat of the waiting limousine and swung in beside her. 'We have to wait,' he advanced. 'Demitrios is clearing your locker out.'

Ellie noted the finality of that statement, but she was past caring. With the slamming of a door, the car moved off a few minutes later. Only when mind over matter appeared to be winning and her stomach had settled back to normality did she risk opening her eyes again. Dio was lounging back in one corner, surveying her with slumbrous dark eyes filled with satisfaction.

'Don't look at me like that!' she told him thinly.

'What way am I looking at you?' he murmured huskily.

The same way she had once seen a man study his new car. With the proud possessiveness of ownership. 'Nothing's changed,' she warned him feverishly.

'Sometimes,' Dio responded with indolent cool, 'you are incredibly naive.'

'On the island. *Not* any more,' Ellie qualified with deliberate acidity. 'And if naive is what you like, well…with your money I'm sure you'll find plenty of takers.'

A slow-burning smile curved his wide, sensual mouth. 'Where would I find a woman with the courage to be as scathing as you?'

'If I were you, I'd be getting worried about what you find attractive in a woman!'

Dio loosed an appreciative laugh. 'You challenge me. I enjoy the fact that you're not impressed by who I am and what I possess. You have no idea how rare a quality that is in my world.'

Ellie tore her attention from the devastating magnetism of his lean dark features, her mouth running dry at the effort even that small amount of self-denial took. She remembered the deference of his relatives at the villa, the invisible boundary line which had enabled him to mix without once being challenged by a more personal approach. His icy reserve had held them all at a polite and formal distance. Only *not* her. Her pride had demanded that she be treated like an equal.

Yet, had she been awestruck and silent around

Dio Alexiakis, she would not now be facing potential disaster, Ellie conceded heavily. If she *was* pregnant, how on earth was she going to cope? Ellie's careful plans for her future had not catered for the possibility of a child. Indeed, those plans had revolved round the necessity of working very long hours well into the foreseeable future. Servicing a large business loan would swallow up a good deal of the income the shop brought in; increasing profit margins would take both time and further investment. Ellie breathed in shakily and struggled to suppress her growing apprehension. Until she had confirmation one way or the other tomorrow, it was foolish to get herself into a state.

'All of a sudden you're a thousand miles away,' Dio drawled.

Ellie blinked and looked back at him, only then realising that the limo had drawn to a halt.

'Of course, you're exhausted,' he conceded grimly.

'No, I think I might be pregnant.' Ellie blurted out that admission without the slightest forethought.

Dio froze in shock. Indeed 'shock', she noted, was not an excessive word to describe his reaction. Stunned black eyes clashed with hers. His strong bone structure clenched hard and he turned pale beneath his bronzed skin.

'Maybe...maybe I should've worked up to saying it...somehow,' Ellie mumbled, although she couldn't imagine any way in which such a bombshell could be delivered gently. She hadn't meant to tell him, hadn't even toyed with the idea of telling him, but the level of her stress had betrayed her.

In the enervated state she was in, she had left the car and allowed herself to be pressed across an imposing entrance hall and straight into another lift before she actually registered that she was not where she had expected to be.

Ellie frowned in bemusement. 'You *said* you were taking me home...'

'I thought we'd be more comfortable at my apartment,' Dio imparted.

'You called *me* sneaky. I don't know where you get the nerve,' Ellie remarked brittly.

All of a sudden every silence simply screamed. She didn't want to think about what she had impulsively blurted out in the limo. She definitely *didn't* want to talk about it. What had she expected from Dio? In this scenario a trouble shared would not mean a trouble halved.

Dio lived in the penthouse apartment. A Greek

manservant ushered them in to the high-tech interior. Seeming acres of space ran in every direction. The furniture was stark and elegant, an effective backdrop for what appeared to be an extensive and fabulous art collection. She focused on one canvas. It looked like a Picasso she had once seen in a book. She realised that it might well be the real thing. Swallowing hard, she looked away again, suddenly utterly intimidated by her surroundings.

'I want to get changed,' she said stiltedly.

Dio showed her into a luxurious guest room. Ellie peeled off her overall and her canvas shoes. She freshened up in the bathroom, noting in disgust that her hands were trembling. She tipped her clothing out of the bag which Demitrios had removed from her locker. After wriggling into her stretchy short black skirt and fine short-sleeved sweater, she hauled on her knee boots. She left the overall lying in a heap. No way would she ever be walking back into work at Alexiakis International again. There were plenty of other evening jobs available…only few of them would be suitable for a pregnant woman.

On her reluctant passage back to rejoining Dio, Ellie noticed a large gilded photo on prominent display on a cabinet in the hall. The photo was of three people. Dio with a tall, older man, so like himself that he simply had to be his late father, and Helena Teriakos, all of them wearing evening dress. The Greek woman had signed it across one corner.

Realising that she was only putting off the inevitable confrontation, Ellie breathed in deep, smoothed down her skirt and walked back into the airy drawing room. She started speaking before Dio even got to turn round to face her.

'I didn't mean to tell you. It was stupid. I'm going to do a pregnancy test tomorrow,' she shared tautly.

Dio swung round. 'You've made an appointment with your doctor?'

'No—'

'I'll make one—'

Ellie stiffened. 'That's not necessary.'

'I think it is,' he contradicted steadily. 'A medical examination would give a more reliable result.'

Ellie folded her arms in a defensive motion. 'But I—'

'I'm as much involved in this as you are,' Dio spelt out stubbornly.

No, she thought strickenly, he *wasn't*. She could feel the distance in him already. He was saying the right things, going through the motions of being decent and supportive, but naturally he was praying hard for a negative result and probably wishing he had never set eyes on her. 'It's very stuffy in here,' she said tautly. 'Can I go out on the balcony? I could do with some fresh air.'

'It's very cold tonight.'

'So shut the doors after me!' Ellie advised sharply.

Dio swept up a remote control. The wall of glass glided back. Ellie headed out with alacrity and was totally unappreciative of his magnificent view of the Thames. She gripped the rail girding the parapet until her knuckles showed white. All she could see in front of her still were Dio's cloaked dark eyes. Those beautiful midnight-dark eyes that haunted her dreams. She heard him behind her.

'Oh, go inside, for heaven's sake!' she urged without turning her head. 'I know you're freezing.'

'I'm not—'

'Look, I boiled alive when you switched off the air-conditioning at the beach house in the middle of the night! We don't even match temperature-wise,' Ellie completed accusingly, swallowing back the thickness in her throat.

'Ellie...' Dio released his breath in an audible

hiss and closed his arms round her, easing her slight body back into the lean, hard strength of his.

Every fibre of her longed to luxuriate in that physical contact, but she gritted her teeth and held herself rigid, refusing to give way to her own weakness. She loved him; she really, *really* loved him. It was a waste of time hoping that those feelings were about to magically go away and leave her free of pain and vulnerability. He wasn't in love with her. At most all Dio had wanted was a casual affair, and now he probably didn't even want that. Unlike Cinderella, she had blown it. She hadn't gone home alone at midnight.

'You feel like ice.' Dio ran long gentle fingers down over her bare arms. 'Come inside.'

'I just want to go home,' she enunciated with great care.

'Not tonight. You shouldn't be on your own.'

'Don't be wet. I've been on my own for a long time.' She hesitated. 'I really shocked you again, didn't I?'

'What do you mean?'

'What I said to you on the beach that night. You just *don't* expect bad things to happen to you.'

'That is not at all how I would describe this situation.' Losing patience, Dio closed a determined arm round her and urged her back indoors. 'You need something to eat.'

Pulling free of him, Ellie sank down on a sofa. 'I'm not hungry.'

Dio sent the wall of glass gliding shut again in the teeth of the wind. He tossed the remote aside and studied her with black fathomless eyes. 'What happens happens, *yineka mou*,' he murmured wryly.

'You still didn't think it was going to happen to you.' Ellie felt like a dog with a bone she had to keep on digging up, even though she knew she ought to leave it buried.

His expressive mouth quirked. 'I have to admit that I am so accustomed to more experienced women who protect themselves from pregnancy that I didn't quite compute the true level of risk we faced.'

'Why do you keep on saying *we*? It leaves me cold,' Ellie told him thinly. 'After all, we don't have a relationship.'

'You are *very* angry with me.'

Colliding with far too perceptive dark eyes, Ellie flushed and squirmed. There was a kind of rage inside her desperate to break out, but he had recognised it before she had.

'Come here...' Dio urged with the sort of rueful exasperation an adult employs with a difficult child.

Ellie could feel a giant well of tears gathering behind her eyes. Instantly she scrambled upright. 'It's late, and if I'm staying, I might as well go to bed...it's not like you're going to make a move on me *now*, is it?'

'Not without a whip and a chair,' Dio agreed with dulcet cool.

Ellie moved a couple of steps away and then paused, discovering that she was oddly reluctant to leave him. 'I thought you'd be punching walls and swearing by now,' she confided without turning round.

'Public school followed by so many years in business teaches a reasonable amount of self-control,' Dio advanced with gentle irony.

'Well, the Mr Smooth and Cool act really annoys me. You haven't given me one genuine emotional reaction since I told you!' she condemned grittily.

But even as Ellie voiced that accusation she saw how foolish it was. How could he give her a genuine reaction? Did she really want him to show her the volatile flipside of that cool, controlled façade which he had donned like armour? *Yes*, she acknowledged. She needed a good excuse to hate him. Everything would be so much more bearable if she *hated* him.

Closing his hand over her knotted fingers, Dio spun her back to him. Ellie dropped her head, struggling desperately to control her emotions. Dio turned her face up to his and met defiant green eyes that shimmered with unshed tears.

A roughened groan escaped him. 'You're panicking. Why? You are not alone with this. Trust me.'

'How do I *trust* a guy who asked me to be his mistress?' Ellie demanded with raw, incredulous force.

'What has that got to do with this?' Dio asked with a frown.

'Everything!' Ellie condemned unevenly. 'You were thinking of what suited *you*…you certainly weren't thinking about my wellbeing! Do you honestly think I'm stupid, Dio? How could I possibly trust you? If I'm pregnant, your solution will be a discreet termination…exactly what my loving father planned for *me*!'

His hard, bronzed features froze. As a ragged sob broke from Ellie's throat, her vision of him mercifully blurred and she twisted away. With a stifled expletive in his own language, Dio closed his arms round her. She made a frantic effort to pull free, but he was so much stronger she might as well have been trying to break through solid steel bars.

Ellie finally subsided against him, weak as water after that outburst which had come from the very depths of her. Crushed against his chest, she listened to the solid, reassuring thump of his heart and drank in the achingly familiar scent of him. She shut her eyes tight and wished the world could stop for ever at that moment.

'I can promise you that I will not suggest *that* as a remedy,' Dio breathed, his Greek accent very thick.

The tight knot of fear inside her began to uncoil. 'I just don't want that pressure put on me...it's not fair,' she muttered shakily.

'At least your mother withstood that pressure—'

A humourless laugh was dredged from Ellie. 'Only because she was terrified of what the procedure might involve.' She snatched in a jagged breath. 'She didn't even *see* that my father just didn't want me to be born. He told her that he couldn't bear the thought of her having to live as an unmarried mother and she believed him.'

'You never did tell me the rest of that story.'

'There was no happy ending.'

'So?' Dio challenged, his deep-pitched drawl reverberating through his chest, making her quiver in reaction.

Ellie lifted her head and looked up at him. It was a long way up, but those stunning black eyes of his could have gripped and held her at a hundred yards. She fought to concentrate. 'Mum was his mistress for sixteen years...'

Taken aback by that bald admission, Dio expelled his breath in a fracturing hiss.

'So you really weren't on a winning streak with that offer you made,' Ellie pointed out, a pained attempt at a teasing smile curving her soft full mouth. 'But at least you're not someone else's husband, like he was...'

Dio had gone very still. His incredible lashes lowered to screen his gaze.

'And even though it wasn't what I wanted to hear, I guess you were honest,' Ellie conceded jerkily. 'Which *he* never was.'

Tension snaked through Dio's big powerful frame. His arms tightened round her. Ellie felt whole again for the first time since she had left Chindos, but all the more conscious that the emotional hold which Dio had on her was stupendously strong.

Dio smoothed the tumbled silvery hair from her damp brow, his eyes liquid dark with emotion. 'You were right,' he murmured with a roughened edge to his dark, deep voice. 'When I asked you to be my mistress, I didn't consider you. I wanted you back in my bed. That was the bottom line.'

Ellie trembled, defenseless against her own hunger to be as close to him as his own skin. 'Well, I don't want to be your mistress,' she whispered shakily. 'But I *do* want to be with you tonight...'

Dio wasn't quite quick enough to hide his surprise.

Shocked by her own daring, Ellie reddened, not even sure where that frank confession had come from.

'I really *don't* deserve you,' Dio grated quietly as he bent and lifted her easily off her feet and up into his arms.

Ellie buried her hot face in his shoulder and gloried in his physical strength. At that instant being with Dio was all she wanted in the whole wide world. He settled her down on a divan in a low-lit elegant bedroom. He ran the zips down on her boots and eased them off. He sprang upright again with that fluid grace she adored and began to undress.

Watching him discard his clothes, Ellie was weak with longing. She shimmied out of her tights and clumsily tugged off her sweater.

'Stop it,' Dio scolded with shimmering golden eyes full of mingled reproach and anticipation. 'I want to do that.'

Her mouth ran dry as he came back to her, his bold arousal flagrant proof of his powerful masculinity. He was like a bronze sculpture, but far too erotic to ever be put on public view. Nor could any metal ever have portrayed his sheer vibrance. Stinging sexual awareness shot through Ellie like an electric current.

Dio unclipped her bra. Her full breasts were adorned by pouting pink nipples. His slumbrous eyes burning her temptingly exposed flesh, Dio suddenly groaned, '*Cristos*…I shouldn't be doing this!'

Ellie frowned in bewilderment. His tension pronounced, Dio raised his scorching gaze to her moist parted lips and then to her confused eyes. Just as suddenly he appeared to reach a decision, and he closed his hands over hers to haul her all the way into his arms. He possessed her mouth with a raw, hungry heat that provoked a startled gasp from her, and then he eased her over him to deftly dispose of the rest of her clothing.

'I want you *every* way there is,' he intoned, lowering her to the pillows and running sure hands over the straining sensitivity of her breasts. 'But gently, *pethi mou.*'

Excitement already running like fire through her as he teased her prominent nipples, Ellie could only manage a shaken moan, and then she reached up, plunging her fingers into his thick black silky hair to draw his gorgeous mouth back to hers again. She let her fingers slide down over his taut flat stomach, reveling in the sudden tightening of his muscles as she traced the fine furrow of hair to its magnificent source.

With a ragged laugh at her new boldness, Dio flung himself flat on the bed and watched her explore him with golden eyes full of indulgence. Then he drew her up to him with lazy eroticism and began to show her what he liked. And, shy and uncertain as she was, she was driven by the most intense need to give him pleasure.

'Enough,' Dio groaned all too soon, lifting her up to him with powerful arms and kissing her breathless. He studied her with deeply appreciative eyes. 'I love teaching you…but you're too fast a learner.'

'Am I?' Ellie shivered, shockingly aroused by the excitement of touching him, loving him. She sank down on his lean, hard all-male length to lose herself in another carnal kiss with the ease of a programmed doll.

He rolled her over and began to systematically drive her wild. Her heart hammered like crazy. Nothing existed for her but Dio and the tormenting need which now controlled her. He found the swollen, aching sensitivity at the very heart of her and she couldn't stay still. Her breath sobbed in her throat then as she twisted and jerked beneath a tidal wave of exquisite sensation.

'Please…' she gasped helplessly.

Eyes burning pure gold, Dio slid between her parted thighs and entered her with an earthy growl of satisfaction. The feel of him stretching her gave her the most intense tormenting pleasure. He moved fast and deep, and a low, keening sound was wrenched from her. His every thrust burned her with liquid fire. All control was decimated, her overwhelming hunger driven higher and higher. She clung to him in wild abandonment, out of her senses with pleasure long before he pushed her to a shattering climax.

Ellie came back to herself with tears in her eyes and a dazed sense of wonder. She relived the instant when Dio had shuddered over her, reaching down his own zenith with dominant power, and she stroked loving fingers through his tousled damp hair and pressed her reddened mouth reverently against his shoulder. 'You make me feel so special...' she whispered unsteadily.

Really special, for the first time in her entire life, she realised ruefully—just as the phone by the bed buzzed and Dio's long, lithe length suddenly tensed above hers.

'Don't answer it,' she muttered urgently, not wanting anything to intrude.

'I'm expecting a call.' Dio eased free of her to roll over and reach for the phone.

Lying on her stomach, Ellie watched him recline back against the padded headboard. His brilliant black eyes were screened from her but she could feel his sudden distance like a cold chill in the air. He was talking in Greek, his darkly handsome features grave and taut.

Ellie frowned, anxiously wondering what the call was about.

A couple of minutes later, Dio cast the phone aside. 'I need a shower, and then I might work for a while,' he announced, his stunning eyes veiled, his jawline clenched. 'Try to get some sleep, Ellie.'

When he sprang off the bed without another word, Ellie paled. 'What's wrong?'

'Nothing that need concern you.'

'Maybe you'd just like me to vanish in a puff of smoke now!' Ellie exclaimed rawly.

Dio drove exasperated fingers through his hair and swore long, low and viciously in his own language. Black eyes glittering, he drew in a deep, shuddering breath, visibly attempting to control a temper that was now, it seemed, on a hair trigger. 'Ellie, just lie down and go to sleep—'

'I'm going home.' Her face a furious pink, but her eyes mirroring her pain and confusion, Ellie swung her legs over the edge of the bed.

Dio loosed a savage groan. 'I *want* you to stay!'

Ellie flung back her head in challenge. 'It doesn't feel like it.'

'I'm not about to beg, *yineka mou*,' Dio incised in stark warning.

It was the endearment that soothed her. At least she assumed that the thing he'd called her was a term of affection. She listened to the shower running in the bathroom, but all happy contentment had now been wrested from her. Maybe he had got some bad news during that phone call. But if that was true, why hadn't he just said so? Her insecurity level began to climb. Inevitably she started questioning the renewed intimacy she had personally invited, and her misgivings mushroomed.

In a desperate need to convince herself that they *did* have a relationship, she had just thrown herself at Dio. All right, she loved him, and was currently suffering from the most humiliating need for reassurance, but that was certainly not an excuse. Tonight, prompted by the fear that she was pregnant, she had tried to attach strings that didn't exist, hadn't she? If Dio was feeling in need of some space now, how could she possibly blame him? She should have resisted her own weakness and slept elsewhere. Why, oh, why did she *always* get it wrong with Dio? she asked herself in positive anguish.

Getting out of bed, Ellie hurriedly gathered up her clothes. She crept down the corridor to the room in which she had changed earlier and climbed into the bed there. If Dio really wanted her with him, he would come and get her. If he didn't— well, then she had done the right thing, hadn't she?

Ellie lay awake for a long time, but Dio didn't put in an appearance to persuade her back into his arms.

Dio's manservant brought her breakfast in bed the following morning. Then Dio called her on the internal phone to tell her that he had made a provisional appointment for her with a consultant gynaecologist willing to see her at noon.

'Nathan Parkes is a personal friend. If you feel uncomfortable with that fact, I'll make other arrangements,' Dio asserted with scrupulous care and tact.

'I don't care who I see,' Ellie responded flatly, worn down by her sleepless night and thoughts that overflowed with regret and self-loathing.

She was impervious to Dio's every impossibly smooth conversational sally on the drive across London. A pretence of polite cool was beyond her. She might love him, but just then she hated him for succumbing to her moment of weakness the night before. Succumbing with enthusiasm and *then* making her feel ten times worse. She wished she had never met him. She wished it so hard that she said it out loud just as she climbed out of his fabulous sleek black Ferrari.

'I don't wish that,' Dio delivered grittily as he strode up onto the pavement beside her, six foot three inches of aggressive masculinity. 'And neither do you.'

'What do you know about how I feel?' she demanded shakily. 'And why have you got out of your car?'

'Naturally I'm coming in with you—'

'Like heck you are! This is one thing I do on my own!'

Twenty minutes later, Ellie's suspense came to an end.

'You're pregnant,' Nathan Parkes informed her levelly.

'Definitely... That is, without any room for doubt?' Ellie prompted jerkily.

'Definitely. No room for doubt.'

Ellie dropped her head and studied her tightly linked hands. Why had she even bothered to question his diagnosis?

'At this stage, feeling a little sick is normal,' the lanky blond man continued. 'But I'm not entirely happy with your weight. You're quite thin.'

'I've been skipping meals recently,' Ellie admitted grudgingly.

'Nausea does tend to kill one's appetite,' he allowed. 'But try to eat small meals regularly. That often helps.'

Pining for Dio had killed Ellie's appetite, but she kept that demeaning truth to herself.

'You *are* planning to continue with this pregnancy?'

Hearing the edge of concern in that query, Ellie nodded in immediate agreement, but she still didn't look up. She had honestly believed that she was prepared for the news that she was pregnant. Now she was discovering that she hadn't been prepared. She felt shocked, and very scared of the future.

'Excellent,' Nathan Parkes pronounced approvingly.

Ten minutes after that, Ellie stood in the empty waiting room and took several deep breaths to calm herself. From the window, she could see the roof of Dio's Ferrari. As she emerged onto the street, Dio climbed out and strode round the bonnet. His dark, deep-set gaze instantly locked to her pale, strained face.

Ellie stared back at him.

'So we celebrate,' Dio announced, pulling open the passenger door and tucking her back inside his car with hands that brooked no argument.

'Can't you just for once say something *honest*?' Ellie condemned in a tight, taut undertone.

Dio leant in to fix her seatbelt for her. 'We're going to be parents. Personally, I feel that the conception of my first child is a *very* special event. If you have nothing positive to say right now, keep quiet.'

A ragged laugh was dredged from Ellie. Dio swung in beside her and immediately fired the engine into a throaty roar.

Ellie worried at her lower lip. 'How do you *really* feel?' she whispered.

'Shattered…kind of smug…sentimental,' Dio enumerated with husky sibilance, closing his hand over her clenched fingers as they waited at traffic lights.

Her tense fingers loosened beneath the enveloping warmth of his. 'I just feel all shook up.'

'You look very tired. I'll take you back to the apartment and you can sleep.'

'No, I promised Mr Barry that I'd come in as soon as possible…anyway, I need a change of clothes,' she muttered uncertainly.

As the lights changed, Dio released her hand. 'I'd prefer you to remain at the apartment. I have to fly over to Paris this afternoon,' he imparted rather grimly. 'I doubt if I'll make it back before tomorrow evening.'

Dismayed by that unexpected news, Ellie stole an anxious glance at him from below her lashes. His lean, hard profile was taut. But then he had frankly admitted that he was shattered, and he was distinctly pale beneath his Mediterranean dark skin. If she was in shock at the idea of having a baby, why shouldn't he be in shock too?

'I think I'd be more comfortable at home,' she said more firmly.

'When you're my wife, I'll expect you to do exactly as you're told at all times,' Dio murmured without any expression at all.

A stark little silence fell. Ellie's eyes had widened to their fullest extent. She couldn't believe that he had said what he had just said.

'Most especially when I am considering your welfare,' he added gently.

Ellie trembled and compressed her bloodless lips. 'You're not seriously asking me to…marry you?'

'Very seriously,' Dio asserted.

'But we hardly know each other—'

'We know enough. I like you. I respect you. I desire you. What more is there?'

'What about…love?' she prompted, striving for a detached tone.

'What about our child?'

Ellie lost colour.

'I *want* to marry you,' Dio told her with quiet emphasis.

'Not really, you don't. People don't get married these days just because of an accidental pregnancy,' Ellie protested unsteadily, her heart beating very fast.

'People like me *do*.'

Ellie swallowed hard. 'Dio, I—'

'You know it makes sense.'

'Yes, but—'

'We'll get married as soon as I can arrange it,' Dio incised with finality.

'I'll think about it,' she returned unevenly.

Dio shot the Ferrari to a halt in front of the bookshop. Unsnapping her seatbelt, he reached for her, black eyes glittering. 'You should be ashamed of yourself, *yineka mou*,' he told her. 'Just *think* about it? Yet only last night you couldn't *wait* to—'

'*Dio!*' Ellie gasped, with a sound between an embarrassed laugh and a shaken reproach.

'So either you're a wanton hussy who shamelessly used me for sex…or a decent woman with a delightful inability to resist me.'

Ellie went pink, but she was wholly mesmerised by his proximity. Involuntarily, she raised a hand, and with her forefinger traced the surprisingly forbidding curve of his wide, sensual mouth. 'I can't…you know it too,' she acknowledged, utterly desperate for him to kiss her.

But, in spite of their proximity, Dio held back. 'I'll call you tomorrow.'

As he freed her again, Ellie blinked in a daze. Dio wanted to marry her? Dio was *willing* to marry her, she rephrased. 'I can't let you marry me!' she said abruptly.

'I won't marry an argumentative woman.'

'Don't tease about something so serious,' she pleaded.

His strong bone structure set hard. 'You and I… it would work,' Dio intoned, his accent thickening.

'Yes…but could you be happy?' Ellie pressed, her whole being centred on the awful wounding necessity of asking that question when all she really wanted to do was drag him off to the nearest church.

Dio groaned in frustration. 'Obviously I should

have proposed over a romantic dinner, with flowers and a ring—'

Ellie winced. 'No, that sort of stuff isn't important.'

'Then my proposal must've been excessively clumsy.' Gleaming black eyes rested on her taut, anxious face. 'I want to marry you, Ellie. The only word I need to hear now is yes.'

'Yes...' Agreement escaped from Ellie before she could bite it back.

'Now that wasn't difficult, was it?' His shadowy smile rocked her heart on its axis, and then he turned away and glanced at his watch. 'Now I'm afraid I have to head straight for the airport. I'll be in touch tomorrow.'

'What's wrong with tonight?' Ellie heard herself ask as she climbed out of the car.

'I'll be tied up all evening.'

Hot-cheeked, Ellie nodded, closed her hands together to stop them reaching out to him and forced a smile. 'OK...I understand,' she said, when she didn't really.

His departure seemed so incredibly low-key that she could not quite believe that he had asked her to marry him and that she had agreed.

Concentrating with a mind in a giddy whirl was

far too much of a challenge that afternoon. In the space of an hour she had learned that she was expecting a baby and she had gained a bridegroom. It was too much to take in all at once...

Dio wanted to marry her. Did fairy tales come true? All right, so her father had been a creep, and on that basis she had judged the whole male sex. Only not Dio. Dio had taken her by storm. He didn't love her. But love could grow, she told herself urgently, determined not to pick holes in her own happiness. Happiness was a fragile thing, and Ellie hadn't known much of it. Dio liked, respected and desired her, she reminded herself. All that plus their baby would be enough to build on. She would make him happy. Whatever it took, she would make him the very best wife he could imagine...

At one the following afternoon, a limousine with tinted windows pulled up outside the shop. Ellie grinned, assuming that Dio had got back from Paris sooner than he had thought.

She immediately asked Horace Barry if it would be all right for her to take her lunch break. But a split second later she stiffened in confusion when a female figure emerged from the limousine. A tall svelte brunette sheathed in a pillbox-red suit. Helena Teriakos, she registered in bemused recognition, just as the other woman entered the bookshop.

The Greek woman focused on Ellie with cool dark eyes, her beautiful face expressionless. 'Is there somewhere we can talk in private?' she enquired.

Disconcerted by that disdainful demand, Ellie flushed. 'Sorry, what is—?'

'We can talk in my car.' Spinning round, Helena Teriakos walked back out of the shop, evidently expecting Ellie to follow her.

Ellie hesitated. She didn't like being taken by surprise. Even less did she like being addressed as if she was a medieval serf. But Helena Teriakos was related to Dio, wasn't she? Certainly she had been swanning about that palatial villa on Chindos like a family member of no small importance. There had been that family photograph in Dio's apartment as well. And if Helena had suddenly taken the trouble to seek her out, it could only be because she knew that Dio had proposed and she had something to say on the subject.

Ellie lifted her jacket, slid into it and went outside. The chauffeur ushered her into the rear of the opulent vehicle. Ellie was very tense.

Helena Teriakos studied her with narrowed eyes and slowly shook her beautiful head in apparent wonderment. 'A shop assistant and a cleaner! Dio really *must* have been distraught that night on Chindos! I confess that I wasn't pleased when he showed up with you at his father's funeral, but in the circumstances, I was prepared to overlook that small social indiscretion—'

'Social indiscretion…?' Ellie queried flatly, her skin reddening beneath that derisive attack. She lifted her chin. 'Why should you have to overlook anything Dio does?'

The Greek woman elevated a brow. 'Men will be men. I'm fond of Dio, of course, but I don't have a jealous temperament. I'm not a sexually possessive woman either. I have always expected Dio to have a mistress after our marriage—'

'*Your* marriage?' Ellie interrupted incredulously.

Helena Teriakos appraised her bewildered face and shaken eyes and laughed with sudden amusement. 'You really *didn't* know, did you? Dio and I were practically betrothed in our cradles. We have known all our lives that we would eventually marry—'

'No…' Ellie broke in shakily. '*No*, it's not true! Dio would have told me….' And then her voice just faded away into nothingness as she recalled that conversation on the beach.

'Why should he have told you? You were just one more in a long line of little amusements, none of whom were destined to be of any lasting importance in Dio's life,' Helena retorted drily, watching all the remaining colour drain from Ellie's face. 'Had you belonged to our social circle, you would have been aware that our friends and families have been awaiting an announcement of a formal engagement for some time now.'

The mists of sheer disbelief had now cleared from Ellie's mind. She was absolutely gutted, her sense of betrayal immense. Helena Teriakos, whom she had foolishly assumed to be a mere relative! She felt sick with pain and mortification. An arranged marriage. Only Dio had termed it, 'picking one's life partner with intelligence'. *Of course* Spiros Alexiakis had had a bridal candidate in mind when he'd urged his son to marry! And Dio had said, 'I'm not ready yet.' Too busy having a good time with a variety of gorgeous willing women to settle down into matrimony at the age of twenty-nine. But throughout Helena had been waiting patiently in the wings.

'I just don't understand how you could accept

Dio b-being with other women...' Ellie stammered helplessly.

'Dio and I have bonds that you could never hope to understand. We share the same background, status and expectations. We are a perfect match,' Helena informed her with supreme superiority. 'Unfortunately Dio rejoices in a rather touching but very destructive sense of humour. He believes that he has to marry you for his child's sake.'

Aghast that Dio had evidently admitted that she had fallen pregnant, Ellie felt horribly exposed and shamed. 'Dio *told* you—?'

'He flew over to Paris yesterday and spent the entire evening with me. Weren't you aware of that either?' A small scornful smile tilted the brunette's lips. 'Believe me, he was quite devastated by his over-active conscience. However, I am a very practical woman. How much will it cost me to persuade you that an abortion would be in your best interests? Five hundred thousand pounds?'

Ellie gazed back at Helena Teriakos in appalled disbelief.

'One million? I am an extremely wealthy woman and I'm prepared to be generous,' Helena spelt out with icy calm. 'You can always tell Dio you had a miscarriage. I won't even insist that you get out of his life. You can still be his mistress. Believe me, you won't last *five* minutes as his wife!'

'I don't want your money…and I'm not getting rid of my baby,' Ellie asserted strickenly, unnerved by the other woman's total lack of emotion.

'But you can't possibly marry him! Can you imagine the headlines? "Dionysios Alexiakis marries a cleaner"?' Helena suggested with a little shudder of revulsion. 'He's a very proud man. You'll be nothing but an embarrassment to him. And by the time the newspapers have finished hauling out the sordid circumstances of your birth and all your former lovers, Dio will have begun to hate you.'

'What do you know about the circumstances of my birth?' Ellie demanded with a raw edge to her strained voice.

'I know everything there is to know about you, Ellie. Money buys information.' Helena dealt her stricken face a pitying appraisal. 'You're in love with Dio. Thankfully I have never felt the need to indulge myself with such messy emotions. Well, make your choice. If you marry Dio, it'll end in the divorce court. True, you'll get the kudos of being his first wife, but you'll lose him completely.'

'I'm not going to marry him,' Ellie framed numbly.

'Now you're being sensible.' The other woman awarded her a cool smile of satisfaction. 'When you trap a man into marriage, it can only end with him hating you. As for the child—you should learn by your own foolish mother's mistake. It didn't do *her* much good bringing you into the world, did it? All those pathetic years of loyalty, only to be rewarded by the sight of your father marrying a secretary half his age the minute he was free!'

Savaged by that cruel attack out of the blue, Ellie scrambled dizzily up and started to get out of the car. 'I'm not listening to any more of this—'

'The door's locked. I'm not finished yet. I do *not* want you to have this child—'

'My child *is* my business!' Ellie exclaimed in angry distrust. 'Now open this door and stop threatening me!'

With a languid hand, Helena Teriakos signalled her chauffeur. 'Think about what I've said. I make a very bitter enemy, and you will discover that Dio has tremendous respect for me.'

Ellie practically fell out onto the pavement in her eagerness to escape. She hurried through the shop and upstairs to her bedsit. But when she got there the tears didn't come. Instead, the kind of outraged and inexpressible pain which Ellie hadn't felt since her mother's death began to mount inside her.

Dio had not been honest with her. She had been dragged into a situation in which she had no defence but that of her own ignorance. She was pregnant by a man who had been virtually engaged to another woman. She had unwittingly poached on another woman's territory and was now being blamed for the entire ghastly mess which had resulted. As for Dio...as for *Dio*, with his wretched sense of honour and his cold, malicious witch of a future wife—well, Helena Teriakos was welcome to him! And the sooner Ellie told him that, the better she would feel!

CHAPTER SEVEN

ELLIE heard Dio come home. She listened to him exchanging a handful of terse words with his man-servant, no doubt learning that she was waiting to see him. Having come over to his apartment the instant she finished work, she had been awaiting his return for almost two hours.

And Ellie now felt like unstable gelignite. The more inconsistencies she recalled in Dio's past behavior, the more she understood, and the deeper her frustrated pain stabbed.

Dio strode into the airy drawing room, his lean, strong face grim, black eyes flat and unfathomable. He emanated stress and tension like a forcefield.

'I understand that Helena paid you a visit,' Dio drawled icily, immediately knocking the ground from beneath Ellie's feet by admitting his knowledge of that fact. 'It was a very generous act on her part, but only what I have learnt to expect from her.'

Thoroughly thrown by that opening, Ellie

gasped. 'A generous act? Are you out of your mind or just plain stupid?'

Dio stilled, his darkly handsome features emanating a freezing distaste that cut Ellie to the bone. 'She offered you her support and assistance. You were rude and offensive. I did not enjoy having to apologise for your behaviour.'

'Having to apologise for my behaviour...?' Ellie repeated almost incoherently, registering that she had seriously underestimated the older woman. Support and assistance? The abortion package? Helena had clearly got in first with her own version of events, and Ellie wondered why she herself should even care. 'She offered me a million pounds to have an abortion.'

Dio studied her for a full ten seconds with widening black eyes full of sheer, lancing disbelief. 'If you must lie, strive to come up with something more credible and less melodramatic,' he derided harshly. 'Helena would never sink to such a level.'

Silenced by the level of assurance with which he made that claim, Ellie stared back at him with bitter anger. 'You really do deserve her,' she breathed in a stark undertone, two high spots of red banishing her previous pallor. 'And if she's so blasted special, *why* were you with me?'

Dio froze. 'I will not discuss Helena with you, Ellie.'

'What a pity you couldn't award me the same respect!' Ellie bit out, so mad with rage and pain she could hardly get the words out.

A slight rise of colour burnished the slant of Dio's stunning but rigid cheekbones. 'The very least I owed Helena was a frank explanation.'

'But you couldn't even bring yourself to refer to her existence around me. You must have known that I hadn't a clue *who* she was the day of the funeral!' Ellie condemned in an emotive appeal. 'I thought she was just a relative—'

'We are distantly related,' Dio conceded, tight-mouthed.

'How very cosy. No wonder you didn't introduce me to her! That's some kinky, twisted relationship you two have…and if she was a nicer person, I might have pitied her for being that desperate to hold onto you!'

Dio rested glittering dark golden eyes on her that burned like lasers. 'I will not listen to you abusing Helena. You don't understand what you're talking about.'

A torn laugh escaped Ellie. 'And if it's anything to do with you, I never will, will I? But it really doesn't matter any more. I trusted you. I thought you were a free man. I would never have got involved with you had I known about *her*.'

'Helena and I are not lovers,' Dio delivered grimly. 'Before last night I had never actually discussed marriage with her. But there was a strong understanding between our families that at some time in the future we would marry.'

'Why the heck didn't you just marry her when your father wanted you to?' Ellie demanded bitterly.

'I resented the pressure being put on me. I should emphasise that Helena played no part in creating that pressure,' Dio imparted flatly.

Saint Helena, safe on her pedestal of perfection, Ellie reflected sickly. And what had she herself been but a last little fling that night on the island of Chindos? A physical release, a momentary distraction from his grief? 'That night we spent together…you already *knew* you were going to go ahead and marry her.'

'Ultimately I always expected to marry Helena. No matter how much you resent that reality, I *can't* alter it,' Dio asserted with bleak emphasis.

'But you weren't honest with me. You never gave me a choice. I can't ever forgive that. And now that

I do know about her, I find it absolutely disgusting that you were planning to set me up as your mistress before you even married her,' she admitted, with a quiver of repulsion at such naked calculation. 'What's the point of marrying someone you can't even be faithful to?'

Dio threw up both hands in a sudden sweeping gesture of violent frustration. 'The last twenty-four hours have been unadulterated hell for me. I am in no mood to stand much more from you,' he vented rawly. 'Whether you like it or not, Helena is the wounded party in this situation. I have hurt her pride and let her down, but she voiced not a single word of reproach.'

'Yes, she's a very clever woman, much cleverer than I am.'

'Cristos...' Dio blazed back at her. 'How can you be so bloody spiteful? It is *you* whom I am going to marry now!'

Ellie stooped to lift her bag with a trembling hand and then straightened to survey him with eyes empty of all emotion, for she was drained. 'I wouldn't have you as a gift, Dio.'

Dio shot her a look of volatile black fury. 'I swear that I will strangle you before I get you to the altar!'

'I mean it,' Ellie told him quietly, watching a sort of stunned light begin to make inroads into his anger as he absorbed her determination. 'Yesterday I was panicking, and foolish enough to grab at your offer of marriage. But your loyalty is with Helena, not where it should be, and I'm not becoming part of some nasty triangle—'

'You are being totally unreasonable!' Dio condemned harshly.

'No, I'm being very sensible.'

'You are carrying my child—'

'And that's the only reason you asked me to marry you…it's *not* enough.' And, sidestepping him in a sudden move of desperation, Ellie walked swiftly out into the hall.

'There is more than that between us, *pethi mou,*' Dio growled in her wake.

'I can get by without the sex too,' Ellie told him witheringly, although even the sound of that dark, deep drawl pulled at her senses.

'Come back here!' Dio grated. 'This is ridiculous!'

Ellie glanced back at him, her lovely face pale as marble and just about as unyielding. 'No…what was ridiculous was that we ever got together in the first place.'

'Ellie—'

'*Please*, give me some space,' she urged with charged emphasis. 'Don't phone, don't come near me. Maybe when the dust has settled on all this we can talk about the baby…just not now.'

For the next week Ellie functioned on automatic pilot. Locked into the need to conquer her desperate craving for Dio, even when she hated him like poison for hurting her so much, she felt totally detached from the rest of the world.

In spite of her request that he leave her alone, Dio phoned every day. On each occasion she put the phone straight back down again, refusing to speak to him. The truth was that she didn't trust herself yet, even on the phone. She was far too vulnerable.

Finding out about Helena Teriakos had devastated Ellie with guilt, jealousy and mortification. Discovering that Dio trusted Helena infinitely more than he trusted her had literally torn Ellie apart at the seams. How much in touch with his own emotions *was* Dio? Did he even appreciate how much he already cared about Helena Teriakos? Once he had resented the pressure put on him to marry her. Wouldn't it be ironic if Dio was only now truly valuing Helena because he had had to face the prospect of giving her up?

All she herself could ever be to Dio was a very poor second best. If she hadn't conceived, Dio would never have offered her more than a casual affair. 'A little amusement,' as Helena had so succinctly put it. That had made Ellie feel about an inch tall. It hurt even more to frankly acknowledge herself outclassed by the competition. Helena *belonged* in Dio's elite world. Dio could marry the woman his father had selected and feel very good about doing so. A gorgeous, accomplished, intelligent, rich and classy ice cube, who was *fond* of him and didn't even care if he kept a mistress. Maybe a lot of guys would be happy to marry a woman as understanding as that, Ellie reflected with helpless bitterness.

That weekend, Horace Barry's nephew, Joe Barry, phoned to tell her that his uncle had flu and wouldn't be in. Ellie was run off her feet. On the Sunday afternoon she went to see Meg Bucknall, to explain that she wouldn't be returning to her job at the Alexiakis building again.

Meg ushered her into her small cosy front room with a real smile of pleasure. 'You really do know how to get the gossip going into orbit, Ellie. I think you're making a wise decision, though. I'll miss you, but you'd have to put up with some stick if you did come back. Some of the younger girls are just eaten with envy.'

'If they knew how I was fixed right now, I don't think they would be,' Ellie fielded wryly. 'It's all off, Meg…was never really on, to tell you the truth.'

'He's turning night into day at the office right now. Half the top floor staff are having to work the same hours. They look worn out, and I heard them muttering that he's in a really foul black mood—'

'I don't really want to hear about Dio, Meg,' Ellie shared, having paled at those edifying titbits.

'Just one little question,' Mega almost pleaded. 'Did *you* dump *him*?'

Not having expected so personal a question from the older woman, Ellie stared.

Meg flushed guiltily. 'It's just that's what we're all hoping. The word is he's never been dumped before, but he could do with being taken down a peg or two.'

'Meg…it would take an attack with an axe to dent Dio's ego,' Ellie retorted.

A surprise awaited her when she arrived home again. Her employer's nephew, a portly pompous man in his early fifties, was seated in the tiny rear office behind the shop, going through the accounts. Standing up, Joe Barry smoothed his sparse hair back from his brow. Ignoring her enquiry as to his uncle's state of health, he disconcerted her by admitting that he had come over in the hope of finding her at home.

But it was what he had to say next which really shook Ellie up. He informed her that his uncle had retired and that he was now taking charge of the bookshop.

The bottom fell out of what remained of Ellie's world. Struggling to come to terms with the shock of that blithe announcement, she frowned. 'But you already *have* a job.'

'I'm taking early retirement. I intend to plough a good deal of money into remodelling this place. However...' He paused, pursing his lips. 'I'm sorry to say that your services will no longer be required.'

'I beg your pardon?' Ellie practically whispered.

'I have no need for a full-time assistant.'

The silence hung there.

'Are you aware that your uncle had already agreed to sell me the business?' Ellie asked starkly.

Joe Barry dealt her a rather smug appraisal. 'My

solicitor assures me that without a witness or any-thing written you would find it virtually impossi-ble to prove that such a ludicrous agreement ever existed.'

'But that's *not*—'

'My uncle should've told you weeks ago. You can't blame me for the fact that he couldn't face telling you that he had changed his mind,' the older man told her impatiently. 'Naturally he would pre-fer to see the shop stay in the family.'

Ellie held her upper body very stiffly, but her legs were trembling. The prospect of buying the shop had been like a life raft, and now she felt as if she was sinking.

'You'll receive everything due to you, of course. I'm giving you a month's notice,' he continued, 'and I'll expect you to move out of that room up-stairs at the same time. You've never had a ten-ancy agreement, and I require that room for other purposes.'

'I'll be out of here sooner than that,' Ellie framed with bleak dignity.

'Well, I must admit that that would suit me *very* well!'

He had the hide of a rhinoceros. Awarding her a

relieved look, he closed up the books and departed, humming under his breath.

It was only six o'clock. Ellie sank down at the foot of the stairs. Five years of minimal holidays, low pay and all those extra hours keeping up the accounts. And at the end of it? One month's notice. What an idiot she had been, dreaming her stupid dreams! There were other businesses out there, but precious few would be within her financial reach. It was time to take stock and make fresh plans. She splayed her fingers over her still flat tummy, thinking about her baby, trying *not* to think about his father.

She was climbing the stairs when the bell went. With a sigh, she turned back. She looked out of the shop's window and simply did not credit the sight of the male grinning at her. Ricky Bolton.

'Come on, Ellie…open sesame!'

Maybe he would give her a laugh. Dio had been notoriously low on giving her a laugh. Ellie un-locked the door. 'How did you find out where I lived?'

Ricky kept on grinning, all white teeth, suntan and bold blue eyes. He exuded a buoyant conceit as powerful as an aura. 'I stole a look at your personnel file before I moved on. I've been meaning to call by for ages, but you know how it is—'

'So many women, so little time?'

'Yeah, well, I can't help being a hot property!' Ricky ran appreciative fingers through his thick blond hair and then grimaced. 'Well, to be honest, I got mixed up with this real terrifying bunny boiler for a while...'

Ellie found herself smiling warmly. 'Tell me more,' she encouraged. 'What did she want? A second date?'

'Could I, like...come inside out of the cold?'

'I'm not feeling *that* friendly, Ricky. You made a real nuisance of yourself on level eight. I also hear you left under something of a cloud? Am I right?'

'Dead wrong!' he contradicted with another hugely self-satisfied grin. 'Good luck came my way and I rocketed up the career ladder.'

'Are you still in that new position?' she couldn't resist asking, wondering if Dio's forecast that he would be fired even faster had been accurate.

'No way! I got myself headhunted out of there again. It wasn't a safe house, if you know what I mean. Fancy a spin in my company car?'

'I'm pregnant, Ricky.'

His grin fell right off his handsome face. 'You're...*what*? My God, what happened?'

'Well...'

'Flamin' hell, who is this guy? Casanova? Where is he?'

Ellie shrugged.

'It figures. Yeah, well, maybe I'll look you up like...next year or something,' Ricky muttered ruefully. 'Probably never. I'm just not into kids at this stage of my life.'

Helplessly amused, Ellie stood up on tiptoes and kissed his cheek. 'Thank you for being that honest.'

Startled, Ricky laughed and rested his arms down on her narrow shoulders. He lowered his head to murmur with recovering good humour, 'Take it from me, you missed a hell of an experience!'

A split second later, the tall blond was literally wrenched away from her. Ellie stumbled back a step in bewilderment. She was just in time to see Dio throw Ricky up against the wall with a snarled Greek expletive and punch him.

'Stop it!' Ellie screeched, absolutely appalled.

Ricky doubled up, groaning.

'You stay away from her!' Dio roared, hauling

him up again. '*You hear me?* You stay away from my woman or I'll rip you apart!'

Ricky focused on his assailant with enlarged eyes full of incredulous recognition.

'You're behaving like an animal, Dio!' Ellie gasped, shattered by his violent intervention.

Dio released Ricky with a volatile gesture of savage derision. He studied Ellie, dark golden eyes blazing condemnation. 'And you ask yourself, whose *fault* is that? I saw you kissing him—'

'On the cheek,' Ricky grunted as he struggled to try and recover his breath. 'You know, I could make a real killing if I charged you with assault.'

'You do what you like,' Dio ground out with magnificent unconcern, still glowering at Ellie full force.

'And an even bigger killing if I went to the tabloids with this extraordinary little set-up,' Ricky mused.

'You deserved a good thump for flogging that tip-off you overheard!' Ellie told him roundly.

Dio froze. His arrogant dark head turned slowly. 'This...*this* is Ricky Bolton?'

'Yeah, you're right, we're definitely evens...' Ricky decided out loud, and displayed his innate survival skills by hurriedly backing into his car. He was gone within a minute.

Ellie shivered in the night air. But even though she was shaken and furious her eyes clung to Dio. His black hair gleamed beneath the street light, accentuating the hard edges of his taut bone structure.

'Ricky Bolton!' Dio suddenly seethed through gritted white teeth. 'What the hell was he doing here?'

'Oh, *please*!' she moaned. 'He just called by. And I don't care what you *think* you saw. You had no business acting like a thug!'

'*Cristos!* How do you think I felt, seeing you wrapped round another man?' Dio growled. 'You told *me* to stay away. You're treating *me* like a leper. I've had just about all I can take!'

Perhaps for the first time since she had learnt that she was carrying his baby, Ellie faced the fact that Dio was under stress as well. Dio had made instant decisions when her pregnancy had been confirmed. Without hesitation Dio had asked her to marry him and had flown over to Paris to explain the situation to Helena. But Ellie had then rejected his matrimonial solution, refused to see him or speak to him and had withdrawn to wallow in her own bitterness. But now she felt guilty. Dio had a right to know where he stood and what was going to happen next.

'I just don't know what's going to happen next,' Ellie confided raggedly.

'I do…' Dio breathed, reaching for her with determined hands and raising her up to crush her startled mouth under his.

That fiery demanding kiss knocked Ellie sideways. His raw hunger snapped her control, released all the seething emotions she had been trying to control. Her head spun; her heart thundered. Sexual heat zapped her. She quivered, locking her straining body to the hard muscle and power of his, a needy moan sounding deep in her throat as she clutched feverishly at his shoulders.

Dio flung back his head, brilliant eyes burning like fire now as he scanned her bemused face. 'You *do* bring out the animal in me, *pethi mou*,' he husked, backing her indoors again and setting her back down on her own feet. 'Where's the alarm system?'

Ellie was still in another world entirely, her body throbbing with the pangs of denial. 'The…*alarm*?'

Dio located it for himself, set it, and doused the lights. Stuffing her bag into her hands, he tugged her outside again and locked up. 'What are you doing?' Ellie finally muttered in bewilderment.

'We're going to have dinner and talk.'

'But I'm not dressed—'

'You've got clothes on, haven't you?' Dio cut in with very male impatience.

Ellie frowned down at her skinny-rib cardy, long black skirt and flat boots.

'You look great,' Dio told her without looking at her as he pressed her into the Ferrari.

Their corner of the quiet, exclusive restaurant was so peaceful and so empty it was as if an exclusion zone had been set around their table. There didn't seem to be any other diners. Ellie lifted her glass of wine.

Dio looked at her, transfixed. Then he reached across the table and literally snatched the glass right out of her hand. 'You can't have that!'

Ellie gazed back at him in total bemusement. 'Why not?'

'You're pregnant. It's safest to stay off alcohol. Don't you *know* that?' Dio demanded.

'Why should I know that?'

'You're a woman—'

'*So?*'

'You're supposed to know about that sort of stuff,' Dio told her with a frown.

'Well, I don't! I'm twenty-one, single and goal-orientated…at least I *was*,' Ellie muttered darkly. 'Why would I ever have been interested in knowing what a woman should and shouldn't do when she's pregnant?'

'As it happens…Nathan dropped this book for expectant fathers in with me.' Dio shrugged, and then shrugged again with exaggerated cool to combat her now widening eyes full of wonderment. 'I just flicked through it.'

Ellie could tell he had read every sentence, down to the fine print. She was touched. He had made more effort than she had and she worked in a bookshop. Maybe he wasn't as squeamish as she was.

'I thought there were things I should know—'

'You really do want this baby, don't you?' she conceded grudgingly.

His dark, deep-set eyes narrowed warily. 'Only if you come as part of the package.'

'What's that supposed to mean?'

'That the way you've been behaving I don't know what to expect any more. You don't want to be pregnant. You don't want to be with me…except in bed,' Dio outlined with a sardonic look of challenge.

An unexpected surge of tears stung the backs of Ellie's eyes. She blinked furiously. 'That's not true...I do want the baby...' she sniffed. 'Oh, for heaven's sake, why am I crying?'

Dio reached for her coiled fingers. 'Your hormones are all over the place right now. It's making you very emotional.'

Ellie reddened furiously and yanked her hand out of his, no longer touched by the prospect of the knowledge he had imbibed on her behalf. 'Did your book tell you I was a brick short of a full load?'

'No, it told me to be understanding and supportive,' Dio imparted piously.

'You haven't got the tact,' Ellie informed him dulcetly.

A slashing smile of amusement curved Dio's beautiful mouth.

Her heart skipped an entire beat. He was so gorgeous she couldn't take her eyes off him.

'I still want to marry you,' Dio delivered. 'But if you've got a better solution, run it by me...just as long as it doesn't entail my baby in a basket behind a shop counter.'

'No, it won't entail that.'

'Leaving him or her to go out to work?'

Ellie squirmed. 'Well—'

'Denying my financial support?'

'Dio, I—'

'No, you listen to me,' Dio asserted forcefully. 'If we don't marry, this child will be an outsider to my family. He won't be a secret. But he's not likely to thank you for making him different from the children I will eventually have *within* marriage with someone else.'

Ellie subsided like a burst balloon. For someone else read Helena. Helena, who would loathe Ellie's child if he or she came visiting. Helena, who would be the ultimate wicked stepmother, determined to humiliate and denigrate the illegitimate outsider. Ellie's tummy curdled, all appetite vanishing. She reckoned even the baby was taking a panic attack at the threat of such a future.

'Something I said *finally* clicked with you?' Dio murmured silkily.

Dredging herself from that nightmare series of visions, pressing a trembling, apologetic hand to her tummy in newly maternal protectiveness, Ellie muttered between gritted teeth, 'Maybe I was a bit hasty saying I wouldn't have you as a gift.'

'That was beautifully put, *yineka mou*. So we're getting married again, are we?' Dio enquired smoothly.

Ellie swallowed hard, humble pie beckoning, and took off defensively on another tack. 'You won't believe what I told you about Helena Teriakos.'

'No,' Dio conceded levelly. 'I could lie to you for the sake of peace, but I won't. Naturally I understand that you were pretty upset that day. You didn't know about Helena but *she* didn't realise that. Had she been aware of it, she would never have approached you.'

Ellie compressed her wobbly mouth. It was obvious he was never going to believe her version. He had known Helena all his life and his trust was absolute. How would she live with that?

'Ellie…the night before you found out that you were pregnant, I made the wrong decision. I didn't think it would be a good idea to start telling you about Helena.'

'You might never had had to tell me.'

Dio left that speaking comment alone, black eyes semi-screened. 'You were under sufficient strain. In any case, Helena was an issue I had to deal with alone.'

'You feel very guilty about her,' Ellie breathed tautly.

Dio frowned. 'How else could I feel?'

Ellie averted her eyes. 'Do…do you love her?' she dared in a driven whisper, and then sat there in mute terror of his response.

'What does love have to do with it?'

That silenced Ellie. It told her so much and yet it told her nothing. Whether he loved Helena or not, he would marry Ellie because she was expecting his child. But how *long* would he stay with her? Would Helena be proved right? But what did she herself have to lose? She would be Dio's wife, for a while at least. Their child would be born legitimate. These days a lot of people didn't seem to set much store by that, but it meant a great deal to Ellie, whose own father had refused to own up to her very existence.

'We put the baby first. Then we worry about us,' Dio spelt out then, with finality.

It sounded like a leading recipe for disaster to Ellie. But the bottom line for her at that moment was that she loved him, and when he got that brooding darkness in his eyes it scared her and made her feel shut out.

'I'd like to get married in a church,' she announced breezily. 'In a totally over-the-top dress. So if you're planning on a register office, you've got no hope!'

Dio's wide, sensual mouth eased into a smile. She felt like a performing clown, but that smile warmed her like the sunshine and she was defenceless against it.

CHAPTER EIGHT

Six weeks later, Ellie walked into her local church, where she was a regular worshipper, to become Dio's wife.

She wore an elegant, fitted, off-the-shoulder dress in palest cream, the superb fabric exquisitely beaded and embroidered. In one fell swoop she had virtually emptied her bank account of five years of savings. It had been like an act of faith in their marriage. She had used one of the credit cards Dio had given her to buy the matching shoes and all the other trappings.

She walked down the aisle alone, and quite unconcerned.

'Someone has to give you away,' Dio had told her on the phone from Geneva, where he had been attending a conference.

'Forget that…what do you think I am? A commodity?' Ellie had demanded. 'I'm almost a twenty-first-century woman!'

'Why did twenty-first-century woman say no to me the night before last?' Dio had enquired silkily.

A squirming silence had fallen at her end of the line.

'I want our wedding night to be special. You *said* you understood,' Ellie had reminded him uncomfortably, her face burning.

'When I was standing under a cold shower at two that morning, aching like the very devil,' Dio had growled back in charged response, 'I changed my mind.'

It was with that memory foremost in her mind that Ellie smiled with sheer brilliance on that walk down the aisle towards Dio. She was blind to the assembled guests crowding out the church, impervious to everyone but the very tall, very dark and very, very gorgeous guy waiting for her at the altar with his best man. This was her day, her moment, her guy. *Mine*, she thought fiercely. Well, she adjusted then, for as long as she could hold onto him.

The ceremony was beautiful. Ellie drank in every word, required no prompting when it came to taking her vows, indeed got in there fast. Why? At the back of her mind lurked a no doubt ridiculous but nonetheless enervating image of Helena Teriakos somehow stopping the ceremony in its tracks at the eleventh hour. 'I make a very bitter enemy,' Helena had warned. And even as the wedding ring went on her finger, Ellie's skin chilled at that memory.

Unfortunately, it hadn't occurred to Ellie that Dio would invite Helena to their wedding. So it was a shock when she saw the beautiful Greek woman approaching them outside the church.

A vision of perfection in a stunning white suit, Helena glided up, grasped both their hands and murmured with a rather sad smile, 'I am very happy for you both.' Then she paused. 'Ellie, I hope you don't mind, but I have something I really need to ask Dio.'

That touching air of plucky feminine vulnerability which had taken Ellie entirely by surprise worked like a magic charm on Dio. He was drawn off to speak to Helena and Ellie was left alone on the church steps. As the minutes ticked past, Ellie got paler and paler, her tension rising. Their guests were noticing, stealing covert glances at Dio and Helena, commenting. Ellie just wanted to die of humiliation.

The society photographer finally called, 'Mr Alexiakis...*please*!'

And only then did Dio return to Ellie's side.

'She did that *deliberately*!' Ellie condemned helplessly when the photographer had finished.

Dio raised a questioning brow. 'Who? What are you talking about?'

How could he be so obtuse? Ellie was so furious she could have shaken him. 'Helena!'

A silence as thick as concrete spread.

Dio breathed in deep.

'Helena remains a close friend, a very close friend,' he spelt out with what sounded like twenty-five generations of aristocratic ice and breeding backing up his chilling drawl.

'Oh, I believe I've got that message all right,' Ellie whispered tightly.

'Then understand this too. I will not allow you to embarrass either myself or her in public. That's my last word on the subject. Get used to the idea *before* I lose my temper!'

And with that blunt warning Dio turned away to speak to his best man, Nathan Parkes. Ellie quivered with sheer rage. She couldn't believe that Dio had had the nerve to speak to her as though she were a misbehaving child threatening to cause a scene. For goodness' sake, he'd got the ring on her finger and then he'd started acting like some medieval tyrant! Hadn't he seen how utterly inap-

propriate and unnecessary it had been for the brunette to demand his attention in the midst of their
wedding photographs being taken? Evidently not.

As Dio swung back to her again, Ellie threw
back her slim shoulders and lifted her chin. 'You
can't talk to me like you just did, Dio—'

'*Ohi*…no?' Dio countered with dangerous quietness, his tone trickling down Ellie's rigid spine
like the gypsy's curse. 'You've got a lot to learn
about Greek men!'

Frankly, at that moment, Ellie felt she had already learnt quite sufficient. She was fizzing with
fury. But before she could respond in kind, Meg
Bucknall appeared a few feet from them. 'Freeze!'
she begged, and eagerly lifted her camera to take
a picture.

'You look just gorgeous, Ellie,' the older woman
sighed appreciatively. 'You didn't have to invite me
but I'm so glad you did. I'm having a great time.'

'The pleasure is ours, Mrs Bucknall,' Dio responded with a charismatic smile.

'The pleasure has just gone *out* of my day,' Ellie
confided as they climbed into the limousine that
would take them to the reception at the Savoy
Hotel.

'When you're in the wrong, I'll tell you,' Dio countered without a shade of regret.

But I *wasn't* in the wrong, Ellie almost snapped, and then conscience spurred her into questioning that conviction. This was their wedding day. Helena's smooth little power play had embarrassed rather than injured. Possibly in allowing her own insecurity full rein, she herself had overreacted.

'Dio,' she murmured ruefully, green eyes very clear, 'This isn't a very easy occasion for me...'

Dio dealt her a questioning, wary look, her change of approach disconcerting him.

'I didn't realise there would be so many guests and I hardly know anybody here,' Ellie pointed out. 'And all your friends and relatives were expecting you to marry Helena.'

Dio tensed. 'Yes, but—'

'Dio, they wouldn't be human if they weren't wondering *why* you are suddenly marrying me instead...' Ellie coloured. 'And if they're thinking what people usually think at times like this, well, they're dead right where I'm concerned, aren't they? I *am* pregnant! Naturally I feel touchy and self-conscious today.'

Dio closed an unexpected hand firmly over hers, black eyes no longer cool and distant. 'I am proud that you are carrying my baby,' he cut in with roughened sincerity.

'So maybe I went over the top about Helena—'

'No,' Dio sighed. 'Once again I was too quick to judge you, and I apologise. I honestly didn't appreciate how you were feeling.'

It was wonderful what difference a little explanation could make. Ellie watched in wonderment as Dio lifted her hand and pressed his mouth softly to the centre of her palm. Her heart seemed to swell inside her chest and her pulse-beat accelerated. A simply huge wave of happiness whooshed up inside her, dispelling all anxiety and unease.

'Even worse, you have no family here of your own to support you,' Dio conceded grimly.

'Mum would have loved all this...' Ellie's smile of acknowledgement was rather tremulous at that emotive thought.

With a rueful groan, Dio pulled her all the way into his arms. 'When you said I had no tact, you hit the target!'

Ellie knew better than to remind him of his father. She hadn't the slightest doubt that the late Spiros Alexiakis would have been anything but happy to see his only son marrying someone as ordinary as she felt herself to be. On the face of it, she conceded painfully, Helena would have been so much more suitable. She rested her cheek against his broad shoulder, the warm, intimate scent of him doing the wildest things to her senses.

Dio glanced down at her, dark, deep-set eyes burning gold. 'Have you ever made love in a limo?' he enquired thickly.

Ellie gave him a helpless grin. 'Oh, yeah, Dio... of course I want to walk into the Savoy and greet all these important people with my make-up half off and my hair all messed up!'

'I could persuade you—'

'But you won't. You're going to be a miracle of restraint...until tonight,' she told him unsteadily, her cheeks warming.

Met by Ellie's determined smile as the bridal couple greeted their arriving guests at the hotel, Helena bent to kiss her cheek with cool familiarity, exchanged a light word with Dio and moved on past. The brunette's supreme confidence and control still daunted Ellie.

Dio watched the smile drop right off Ellie's expressive face again. 'Try to appreciate how difficult this must be for her.'

Ellie nodded and flushed, feeling herself rebuked although she had done her utmost to look calm and friendly. She had never been very good at hiding her emotions. And it looked as if she was stuck with the stigma of having lied about what had passed between her and the older woman at their first meeting. But then wasn't it possible that in the heat of the moment Helena *had* acted totally out of character that afternoon? Helena might now regret her behaviour, Ellie thought with sudden hope, resolving to be more generous herself.

Nathan Parkes introduced her to his wife, Sally. She was a bubbly redhead with freckles and a friendly, easy manner. 'I wish I'd got the chance to meet you before the wedding. I did think of asking Dio for your number and calling you. But I knew you'd be frantically busy and I didn't want to seem too pushy.'

'I'd have been delighted,' Ellie told her warmly, since she was beginning to appreciate that the tall, softly spoken gynaecologist was a much closer friend of Dio's than she had initially realised.

'Great. I'm not much good at standing on ceremony,' Sally confided cheerfully. 'And I was really hoping you wouldn't be like—' As she bit back what she had been intending to say, she reddened like mad. 'What I meant to say was…was… we, well—'

Nathan stepped in to rescue his wife from her discomfiture. 'Sally hopes you'll come and stay with us in the country some time soon. We warn our guests in advance—we have a muddy yard, three noisy kids and a manic dog!'

'I'm not a *cordon bleu* cook or anything,' Sally warned rather anxiously.

'I'm not a fussy eater, and I'd be happy to help out,' Ellie said quickly, thinking that their home and family sounded delightful.

Dio glanced at Ellie with a raised brow. '*Can* you cook?' he asked in surprise.

Nathan shot his friend a helplessly amused look and laughed outright. 'Dio, that says it all, it really does! Are you aware, Ellie, that Dio didn't even know how to switch on a kettle when he first came to stay with us?'

'They're a lovely couple,' Ellie whispered when they were eating their meal at the top table. 'Have you known Nathan long?'

'I was in a car smash when I was nineteen. Nathan was doing his stint as a med student in the casualty unit.' For some reason that recollection made Dio's firm lips curve into a surprisingly amused grin.

'What's so funny about that?'

'I only had concussion, but my father was in a highly emotional frame of mind when he arrived.' Dio grimaced. 'He behaved as if Nathan had saved me from certain death and embarrassed the hell out of both of us. I think Nathan agreed to spend the weekend on our yacht just to escape being wept over and embraced!'

'Of course your dad was upset. You were an only child,' Ellie scolded, dismayed even by the mention of a car accident that had happened a decade earlier, simply terrified at the idea of anything ever happening to Dio.

Dio gazed deep into her anxious green eyes and his mouth quirked. 'I wish he'd met you—'

'No, you don't!' Ellie told him roundly. 'He'd have locked you up before he'd have let you marry someone like me!'

'What *is* this "someone like me" stuff?'

'It's my Cinderella complex talking. I certainly don't mean that you're my prince, Dio, so don't be getting a swollen head!' Ellie cautioned. 'You're the guy who first switched on a kettle as an adult… and I was the latch-key kid who got my own tea from the age of seven!'

Dio wasn't amused. 'No damn wonder you find it so hard to lean on me.'

'Most people I've tried to lean on in life fell over!' Ellie joked instantly, hoping to make him lighten up again, wishing she hadn't mentioned her childhood.

'But I won't,' Dio intoned very seriously. 'You have to learn to trust me, *pethi mou.*'

Sometimes men were a tonic, she decided. He had said that without a shade of irony. Yet *he* didn't trust her. At least, her word didn't yet carry the same weight and value as his lifelong friend Helena's, Ellie couldn't help reflecting. But she swiftly suppressed that thought. They were married now, and it was early days yet. Time would take care of that problem. She couldn't see that he would be meeting up with Helena Teriakos very much in the future, and she was too practical to make a running battle of that issue in the short term. A new marriage was a fragile thing. Wouldn't it be foolish to make the beautiful Greek woman a bone of contention?

A few hours later, in the luxurious room set aside for her use, Ellie removed her wedding gown with rueful regret and put on the travelling outfit she had purchased. A loden-green suit, its fitted jacket adorned with snazzy gold buttons and teamed with a fashionable short skirt. It had cost the earth and she had picked it with great care. But the more mature appearance she had initially attempted to strike hadn't come off. Those kind of clothes didn't look right on her yet. She was twenty-one and she didn't look older than her years.

When she returned to the crush of guests awaiting their departure for the airport, she was rewarded by the appreciative gleam that awakened in Dio's expressive eyes the instant he saw her. Her rather anxious smile became downright sunny.

'You look about eighteen. I should be hung,' Dio groaned, but he curved a wonderfully possessive arm round her small thin figure. 'Go on, throw your bouquet.'

'No, I want to keep it.'

'I thought it was tradition.'

'No, I'm having mine preserved and framed… or something,' Ellie told him stubbornly.

The number of people wishing to exchange last words with Dio briefly forced them apart. Ellie watched Dio laughing at some sally, and something akin to pure joy blossomed within her. He really did look happy and relaxed, just as a new husband should look.

And then, from behind her, a cool smooth voice remarked, 'I pity you, Ellie. Playing the whore between Dio's sheets won't hold him for long. And you don't *have* anything else to offer him, do you?'

In shock, Ellie froze, and then she spun round

with a jerk. But Helena Teriakos had already moved on to chat to an older couple some distance from her. However, Sally Parkes was standing only a foot away, her mouth wide, her eyes almost as appalled as Ellie's. 'I was just hurrying over to speak to you before you left. Did I *really* just hear what I thought I heard?' she demanded in an incredulous whisper. 'My goodness, I never thought that cold fish had it in her to be that spiteful!'

That surprising comment dredged a nervous giggle from Ellie. 'Now you know.'

'Go and tell Dio right this minute,' Sally urged her keenly.

'No, I'll handle it myself...' Ellie said awkwardly, mortified colour now banishing her previous pallor. 'I did kind of steal her man, so, well...I can't blame her for hating me.'

Sally Parkes frowned. '*Her* man? They weren't even dating, never mind engaged. Surely you don't believe *she's* been sitting home just waiting for Dio to pop the question! If a richer, more powerful prospect had come along, she'd have married him years ago!'

Ellie felt uneasy. She liked Sally, but, although it was comforting to be told such things, she didn't want to discuss Helena with anyone.

'Honestly!' Sally was into full swing now, venting what were obviously pretty personal feelings about the other woman. 'Helena's all sweetness and light around Dio. I'd just love him to know what she's *really* like! Men can be so blind.'

'Yes,' Ellie agreed, frantically trying to think of a change of subject.

'He's had a real narrow escape. She's the original ice queen and the most awful snob. Nat and I just aren't good enough to share the same room with her!' Sally shared feelingly.

'Who aren't you and Nat good enough to share the same room with?' Dio enquired with amusement. He closed a powerful arm round Ellie as he spoke, only to glance down at his bride in surprise when she jumped in guilty dismay. 'What's wrong?'

'I'm feeling a bit dizzy,' Ellie announced, and right then she genuinely was. Dizzy with apprehension. She was terrified that Sally was about to name Helena and give Dio the impression that they had been enjoying a mutual muck-raking session.

But a split second later she saw that she needn't have worried. Poor, outspoken Sally was hotly embarrassed by Dio's untimely interruption. And, as a distraction, Ellie's plea of dizziness worked a treat. Dio assisted her into the limousine as if she was an elderly lady of at least a hundred and one.

Then he climbed back out again to stride over to Sally's husband, Nathan.

From her stance a few feet from the car, Sally made the most comical grimace of relief. She pretended to mop her brow, evidently as aware as Ellie of Dio's high opinion of Helena and grateful not to have caused offence.

Dio swung into the limousine beside Ellie. 'The instant the jet's airborne, you're going to rest,' he informed her with determination, fresh from what appeared to have been an urgent consultation with Nathan in his professional capacity.

'But I'm OK!' Ellie protested in dismay.

'I should never have invited so many people. It's been a hell of a demanding day for you...and I know it sounds crass but I keep on forgetting that you're a pregnant lady!' Dio told her apologetically.

Actually, no news could have pleased Ellie more. Only by the time she heard it, it was too late. There she was, longing to be passionately kissed, and Dio was behaving as if she had turned into some kind of invalid. When she argued, he simply assumed that she was striving not to be a sickly wet blanket. He then told her off for trying to take such an attitude with him, and pointed out that she had to accept the need to take extra care of herself now.

As soon as the jet was on route to Greece, where they were to spend a couple of weeks, Dio stashed Ellie on the bed in the cabin and helped her out of her shoes. He would have helped her out of her suit as well, but Ellie pulled away.

'Go to sleep,' he urged bossily. 'I know you have to be exhausted.'

'I'm *not*,' Ellie groaned in despair.

Dio crouched down lithely by the side of the bed. Vibrant dark eyes swept her mutinous but pale face. 'Don't you want to be awake for our wedding night?' he murmured silkily.

'I thought Nathan might have put *that* on the forbidden list as well,' Ellie said crossly.

Dio gave her a shimmering smile of amusement and smoothed her tumbled hair gently off her brow. 'You're such a kid sometimes.'

Ellie was so annoyed at that assurance she flipped over to turn her face to the wall and presented him with a stiff back.

'And that's really good for me!' Dio protested with a tremor of laughter disturbing his usually even diction. 'Occasionally I now have to think for two people instead of one. For a male who has been extremely selfish and spoilt for most of his life, that's really terrific therapy!'

'Oh, really?' Ellie muttered sniffily. 'I'm so glad *one* of us is having fun!'

Dio burst out laughing. Ellie flipped back over, real temper sparking, and then she collided with his beautiful dark eyes. Her heart skipped a beat and she totally forgot what she might have been about to snap back.

'I promise you, *agape mou*. The fun will include you tonight,' he swore, not quite steadily.

And only when she was free of the undeniable distraction of his vibrant presence did Ellie feel the heaviness of the exhaustion she had rigorously denied slowly creeping over her to weight her limbs.

'Stop it,' Ellie surfaced to mumble in complaint when she sensed disturbance some timeless period later.

'Hush,' Dio soothed.

Ellie slid a sleepily seeking hand beneath his jacket. She spread possessive fingers across the silk shirt separating her from his warm, virile body and sighed with contentment. Dimly assuming he was lying down beside her, she sank back into peaceful sleep.

She finally wakened and stretched, only find to

herself under restraint. Her eyes flew open. Dio was carrying her. 'What…where?'

'You've slept well for a lady who wasn't remotely tired. You've been out of it for the whole trip,' Dio drawled, with more than a hint of that satisfaction peculiar to a male who enjoys being proved right.

Ellie focused on the familiar frontage of the vast villa he was striding towards. 'For goodness' sake…put me down.'

'I can't. I left your shoes behind on the jet.'

'How on earth did you cart me through Athens airport?' she gasped.

'The same way.' Dio laughed. 'It did cross my mind that the fact you're not as staturesque as Helena was a distinct advantage—I'm still fit to carry you over the threshold!'

Ellie froze at his reference to the other woman, the disconcerting comparison which he had unthinkingly made. Dio tensed, closed his eyes and just groaned out loud, evidently registering what he had just said.

Ellie made an enormous effort. 'It's OK,' she stressed with a forced smile intended to soothe. 'She was part of your life for a long time…I understand.'

As he reached the palatial front entrance of the

villa, Dio sent a rueful glance down at her. 'Until I met you, I really believed I was a skilled diplomat.'

'It's all that boot-licking that goes on around you,' Ellie told him baldly.

'No, it isn't that. It's *you*,' he condemned with a wry light in his eyes. 'I get so used to listening to you say whatever you like that I relax my guard around you.'

Ellie thought about that. 'That's good.'

Well, sometimes it would be good—even most of the time, she adjusted inwardly. But right now she really could have done without finding out that Dio had been comparing her in even the tiniest way with Helena. Such a trivial little comparison too: Helena so tall and shapely, Ellie so small and slightly built. But still Ellie would have preferred not to have had the confirmation that the beautiful brunette was still so much in Dio's thoughts on *their* wedding day.

But then it didn't take a rocket scientist to work out *why* Helena was on Dio's mind. All his adult life, Dio had assumed that Helena would be his wife. He had had little time to come to terms with the sudden switch in brides. And he certainly *cared* about Helena, Ellie was forced to concede. He praised the beautiful brunette, became angry if she was criticised and hotly defended her. As she faced those hard facts head-on, Ellie was in pain. What if Dio really *did* love the other woman? It was perfectly possible that he had decided to put the needs of his unborn child ahead of his own personal feelings. But if he had done that, time would weaken his resolve, wouldn't it?

As they entered the huge hall, Dio dragged Ellie back to the present by momentarily stilling with a low-pitched groan. 'We have company,' he sighed.

Two tiny old ladies with almost identical creased faces and wide smiles were waiting for them in the hall. Ellie rather thought she had noticed the elderly pair in their old-fashioned black dresses on her previous visit to the villa.

Dio greeted both women in a flow of warm Greek. He settled Ellie down on her stocking-clad feet to introduce her to his grandmother's twin sisters: Polly and Lefki.

'Dio has no mother to welcome you to your new home,' Polly—Ellie thought it was—said in heavily accented English. 'We are here to make you welcome.'

'To make you welcome,' Lefki repeated cheerfully.

'Lefki, I have said that.' Her sister turned to admonish her.

'But we are not staying long.' Lefki gave her sister a decidedly defiant look.

Ellie couldn't help herself. She just grinned.

An abundant supper awaited them in the big drawing room she remembered. Polly and Lefki sat perched on the sofa opposite. They were so small and shrunken that their feet didn't touch the carpet. In between arguing with each other, they urged more food on Dio and shot loaded questions at Ellie.

What did she think of the island? With pride, they announced that neither of them had ever left the island, even for a day. Didn't she think it would be a wonderful place to live all the year round? Did she know how much Dio loved Chindos? Didn't she think that Dio worked too hard and travelled too much? Their love and concern for Dio became more endearingly obvious with each word.

When they finally took their leave in an elderly Rolls Royce, driven off at a snail's pace by their careful driver, Dio shot Ellie a slightly uneasy glance. 'Sorry about that. Polly and Lefki live at the far end of the island. I can appreciate that some people find them rather eccentric, but they rarely visit.'

'Oh, I hope not. They're absolutely adorable,' Ellie told him. 'What age are they? Have they always been together?'

'Ninety-two and, yes, they're completely inseparable.' Dio smiled warmly down at her and relaxed. He dropped an arm round her as he walked her up the spectacular central staircase. 'I'm glad you like them. I have a soft spot for my great-aunts. When my mother died, Polly and Lefki were a great comfort to me, and I've never forgotten that.'

He drew her into a fabulous bedroom furnished with the same unashamed opulence as the ground floor. Gorgeous flower arrangements scented the still air. Ellie glanced at the magnificent bed and her tummy clenched with anticipation. She looked away, her cheeks warming, embarrassed by the sensual stirrings of her own body. It was hard to credit that only a few weeks ago she had been blissfully ignorant of how powerful sexual hunger could be.

'I could do with freshening up,' she confided shyly.

'So could I,' Dio purred like a big lazy cat, casting off his jacket and tugging loose his tie.

Watching him strip, she ran out of breath and mobility. Meeting those dark golden eyes, feeling their bold, sensual glide over her taut figure, she felt her heart start to beat very fast. Naked now, his lean, bronzed, hair-roughened length a feast for her wakening senses, Dio strode over to her. He undid the buttons on her jacket one by one and eased it from her shoulders.

'I want to drive you wild,' he told her huskily.

'My imagination has already done that for you...' Ellie confided.

Releasing her bra, Dio curved his hands to the new fullness of her breasts. He smiled with sensual appreciation as she jerked and gasped at the brush of his thumbs over her urgently sensitive nipples. Suddenly intent, Dio pushed her gently down onto the bed. Following her there, he sealed his mouth hotly to a straining pink bud, laving it with his tongue and the edge of his teeth. Fiery response whooshed through her trembling tautness, provoking a driven moan from her parted lips.

Dio raised his dark head again, raw hunger in his eyes. He angled back and skimmed off her skirt. He dispensed with her remaining garments with unconcealed impatience. As he ran his burnished gaze over her pale nudity, she felt as if she was burning all over. 'You are so perfect…I need a shower just to cool off,' he confided thickly.

'Me too…'

In the spacious shower cubicle, she leant up against him beneath the energizing beat of the water. Weak and hungry as her treacherous body was, anxiety still pierced her thoughts. She wouldn't be *perfect* much longer. Her breasts were already fuller. Their baby would soon wreak havoc with the taut, slim figure he liked so much. Her waistline would thicken; her stomach would swell. Would Dio still find her attractive then?

'I'm going to look like a balloon in a few months,' she muttered helplessly, unable to keep her fear to herself.

'Hmm…' Dio sighed, sliding a reflective hand down over her still flat tummy, letting his fingers splay and linger. 'I'm looking forward to showing you off.'

'Showing me off?' Ellie echoed weakly.

Dio sank down on the corner seat and tugged her down on top of him. Angling his handsome head back, he luxuriated in the warm jets of water hitting them from all directions before he looked at her again. A slashing grin slated his wide, sensual mouth then. 'I think it must be a guy thing, *agape mou*. You have my baby inside you. That's a hell of a turn-on.'

'It *is*?' Taken aback by that assurance, Ellie stared at him.

Eyes flaming to molten gold, Dio deftly shifted her so that she sat astride him. With amusement, he watched her register the strength of his arousal for herself.

'Oh...' Suddenly bereft of breath, Ellie found her own hopelessly susceptible body reacting with violent enthusiasm to the sensual masculine threat of his.

Dio cupped her damp cheekbones and took her mouth with a hot, hungry brevity that sizzled through her every nerve-ending. 'So what are we going to do about it?' he husked.

Anything you want,' she whispered, barely able to keep her voice steady.

And, with a hungry groan of satisfaction, he took her at her word. The urgency of his need both shocked and excited her. In the aftermath of her own shattering climax, she was still trembling as he towelled her dry. By then Dio was apologising, and then laughing at the same time.

'Don't you ever tell anyone that our marriage

was consummated in a shower,' he breathed. 'I'd never hold my head up again!'

'Why?'

He laid her down on the magnificent bed. 'I should have been more romantic. It's our wedding night,' he reminded her with a rueful glint in his eyes that had so much appeal it tugged at her heart. 'But the thought of making love without contraception for the first time in my life made me rampant!'

'Rampant works like magic with me,' Ellie confided with a giggle, tugging him back down to her with possessive hands, surrendering to her overpowering need to keep in constant physical contact.

Dio smiled, slumbrous dark gold eyes scanning her with appreciation. 'I like this,' he said softly. 'I like it that we can laugh even in bed. I've never had that before.'

Ellie woke up around dawn. Wandering sleepily back from the bathroom, she paused to study Dio where he lay on the bed, her eyes soft with tenderness and love. The white sheet was tangled only partially round one long, lean, powerful thigh. For a split second she just couldn't believe that he was *her* husband. And then she tossed her silvery fair head back and smiled. The fears she had harboured the night before now seemed remote and rather hysterical.

Right now, her body ached from the hunger of his. He wanted *her*, not just the baby. He wasn't turned off by her pregnancy either. And if he had been feeling trapped into marriage by his own sense of honour, he would surely have been a less keen lover. But Dio had spent the night demonstrating over and over again that he found her very desirable. He had restored her confidence in herself.

Pregnancy had shattered that confidence and hurt her pride. For a while, the status quo had changed, she acknowledged. She hadn't liked that. She had made some mistakes too. Her innate need for reassurance had made her feel dependent and weak, no longer his equal. Now those uneasy feelings were gone and she felt more secure. Sliding back into bed beside him, she sighed. She felt incredibly happy.

A smiling young maid woke Ellie later that morning by opening the curtains. It was after eleven. Dio had gone and she couldn't credit that she had slept so late. Her breakfast arrived on a wicker bed-tray complete with a bud vase. Gosh, this is fun, she decided, resting back against her banked-up pillows feeling like a queen.

After she had eaten, one startled glance at her tousled appearance sent her rushing to the shower. When she had finished drying her hair and had applied a little light make-up, she found that her clothes had already been unpacked and tidied away in the capacious dressing room. She had bought several casual outfits before the wedding, and she put on a cool cotton shift dress in misty pastel shades of mauve.

As she descended the stairs, she heard Dio. Dio…his distinctive voice raised in…*anger*? A short dark young man erupted like a bullet from a doorway at the back of the hall. Awarding Ellie a startled look, he flushed and paused to proffer a strained greeting in Greek before he hurried on past. Ellie frowned in surprise.

Dio was talking harshly on the phone in his own language. He was in an elegant room furnished as an office. His short-sleeved linen shirt and tailored chinos in pale natural colours were a superb frame for his black hair, bronzed skin and sleekly powerful physique. He looked so stunning that for a foolish moment Ellie just hovered on the threshold, watching him stride back and forth like a caged tiger, his every lithe, restive movement screaming ferocious tension.

Ellie's scrutiny finally roamed from the husband she adored to the crumpled tabloid newspaper spread out across the desk. An English Sunday newspaper, she noted, flown out already. Her curiosity was roused as she moved closer.

Slinging aside the phone, Dio swung round and belatedly noticed her. '*Cristos*...what are *you* doing in here?' he thundered in disconcertion.

But it was already too late. Ellie had got close enough to recognise first a photograph of their wedding and then the people in the other smaller photos. Both her parents! There was her father, Tony Maynard, clambering out of his Mercedes, looking hunted and furious. It was the first time Ellie had seen him in over five years. She was paralysed to the spot, the colour draining from her shattered face.

Dio released his breath in a stark hiss. 'I don't think you should read that stuff. It's only going to upset you.'

Ellie stared down at the pages. There was a picture of the shabby street where she had lived as a child. The caption beneath ran, '*From poverty...to wealth beyond avarice. How? The billion-dollar baby!*'

'Oh, *no*...' Ellie mumbled strickenly, her tummy lurching with nausea at the crude shock of such humiliation, in print for all the world to see.

CHAPTER NINE

'SCARCELY the way I would have chosen to announce the advent of our first child,' Dio commented in a charged undertone that fairly screeched with restraint.

'No…' Ellie agreed, trembling.

'But, had you warned me how much scandal there was in your past, I might have been able to bury some of the evidence and protect you.'

Ellie flinched from the censure she could hear in his clipped drawl. And as she read what was in that newspaper article she didn't blame him; she really didn't. It *was* lurid stuff. The barest bones of the truth were there, but sunk beneath a wealth of lies and exaggerations.

'For a start, I had no idea that you and your mother were virtual outcasts in the town where you grew up.'

'Dio…it was a small town. Mum was an unmarried mother when it wasn't at all acceptable.' Ellie cleared her throat of the thickness of tears. 'Her

father died owing money to a lot of local trades-
men. Neither of those facts was going to win her
any popularity contest. And when my father was
seen visiting by the neighbours...well, everyone
knew he was a married man.'

'Why didn't you tell me that he ditched your
mother to marry his secretary a few months after
his first wife died?' Dio enquired drily.

He was concentrating on the revelations about
her background rather than the infinitely more
damaging and cruel comments about her in the
present. She had been branded a cunning little
gold-digger, who had seen her chance with a rich
man and grabbed it with both hands. She felt sicker
than ever.

'Ellie...' Dio prompted curtly.

'Well, to be blunt...Th-that's not one of my favourite memories,' she stammered painfully. 'My
father didn't even bother to tell Mum that he had
another woman in his life. The first she knew
about it was the notice of their marriage in the
local paper! She was devastated.'

'Yes, and I would have preferred to have learned
from *you* that she took her own life.'

Ellie rounded on him in shaken rebuttal. 'She
didn't! She was taking medication for depression.

She was living in her own little world. She stepped off the pavement at a junction without looking and just got knocked down!'

Dio surveyed her with bleak eyes and his hands coiled into fists which he dug into his pockets. 'You were only sixteen. How the hell did you cope alone at that age?'

'My caring father sent his solicitor to arrange the funeral. He didn't attend himself, of course.'

'Then what?' Dio prompted, looking grimmer than ever. 'Why did you leave school?'

Ellie frowned in surprise. 'What choice did I have?'

'At the very least your father should have ensured that you completed your education—'

'Why would he have done that when he had spent sixteen years trying to pretend that I was nothing to do with him? He was scared his wife would find out about me and throw him out. All the money was hers,' Ellie explained wearily.

'So what did you do after your mother died?'

'Our flat was rented. I sold the household stuff to a dealer and went to London. I stayed in a hostel until I got the job with Mr Barry. The year after that, he offered me the room above the shop. Dio, why are we talking about my background?' Ellie studied him with bewildered eyes. 'I didn't tell you any lies. I may have skipped the messier details, but that's no hanging offence.'

His black eyes flared to smouldering gold. 'At this moment, I want to strangle you,' Dio confessed in a wrathful undertone. 'But if we talk about what doesn't really matter for *long* enough, I have more hope of getting my temper under control!'

Ellie frowned in confusion. Was he blaming her for that scurrilous article? How could he? She asked him, certain she had to be wrong.

'Of course I'm blasted well blaming you!' Dio launched back at her, his pent-up outrage unleashed by what he evidently considered to be a very stupid question.

Ellie turned very pale. 'But why?'

'The trail leads back to *you*, Ellie. If I'm not very sympathetic, it's because your own lack of discretion has brought this on us both!' he condemned with raw impatience.

'Lack of discretion?' Ellie echoed blankly.

'Nathan didn't even tell Sally that you were pregnant! He knows she's a hopeless gossip. And now I know I've got a wife who makes his look as secretive as the CIA!' Dio bit out sardonically. 'How many people have you told that you're pregnant?'

'None!' Ellie's temper rose as she finally grasped why he didn't feel she was entitled to sympathy. He fondly imagined that all that information had leaked from her own foolish lips!

'You must have told someone. I would trust Nathan with my life. The press couldn't have managed to put all this together so quickly *without* assistance from someone close to *you*!' Dio spelt out with emphasis.

Ellie then recalled telling Ricky Bolton that she was expecting a baby, and she coloured hotly.

Dio was watching her like a hawk eager to swoop on a tender prey. 'Who *was* it?'

Ellie was thinking at a frantic pace. Ricky might have known she was pregnant, but he hadn't known a single thing about her parentage. Then she stilled, an expression of appalled comprehension slowly freezing her eloquent face. She could not believe what a fool she had been not to grasp who was behind such a vindictive attack on her.

'Ellie...I want a full confession. Then possibly I will calm down,' Dio contended, in not the most convincing of promises.

Ellie scrutinised him in agonised silence. She *knew* that he was likely to spontaneously combust if she spoke the name that already lay between them like a mine-filled stretch of enemy territory. But at the same time she had to defend herself.

'Ellie...' Dio grated.

'You really want to know who I think is likely to have been behind this newspaper stuff...?' Ellie swallowed and tilted her chin. 'In my opinion, the most likely candidate is Helena Teriakos.'

Boulders could have dropped soundlessly into the deep, deep silence that fell. She might as well have named a cartoon character. Dio stared at her with wondering black eyes as if she was intellectually challenged.

'It *has* to be her,' Ellie continued valiantly. 'She already knew about my background and she hates me—'

'Have you taken leave of your wits?' Dio demanded in an almost ragged plea.

Ellie jerked a slight shoulder. 'If it's any consolation, Helena has *you* taped too,' she added, no longer struggling to choose her words with care. 'She said that you were easily embarrassed, and she said that you'd turn on me.'

Dio swept a silencing hand through the air. As a gesture, it was highly effective in its intimidating authority. 'You are so devoured by jealousy you can't see straight, never mind reason rationally—'

'Right at this moment, I am certainly not *jealous*, Dio.' Ellie thrust up her chin as she voiced that reality. 'If Helena came to that front door right now, I'd hand you over without a murmur!'

'That's enough!' Dio growled.

'I'm not finished!' Ellie's anger was shooting higher even as his inexplicably appeared to be on the wane. 'You *deserve* her! I wish you *had* married her. You'd have got frostbite on your wedding night!'

Dio breathed in very slowly and deeply. Then he said, 'I think this could be that stage when the honeymoon phase comes to a sudden very sticky end.'

'I've had enough of you and that malicious vixen,' Ellie announced tremulously.

'Tough,' Dio responded with extreme quietness.

That switch in attitude bemused her. 'What do you mean, *tough*?'

'You're my wife and you're not going anywhere. In fact, while you're displaying this deeply disturbing manic streak where Helena is concerned, you're staying on this island. I have to confess that I literally *cringe* at the prospect of you meeting up with her again. Look at yourself!' Dio invited with a curled lip. 'You're practically jumping up and down with rage as it is.'

'What do you expect?' Ellie screeched so loudly her voice broke.

Dio closed a determined arm round her shivering figure. 'This is not good for the baby—'

'Get your hands off me!' Ellie hissed.

'No, your emotions are running out of control. It has to be your hormone level,' Dio decided, surveying her with extreme gravity but with a definite look of relief at an explanation he evidently liked very much.

'My...hormone level?' Ellie practically whispered.

'In early pregnancy a woman may be prone to emotional changes and may require extra support and understanding.'

Ellie's jaw dropped at what sounded very much like a direct quote from a textbook.

A dark flush scored Dio's stunning cheekbones as he appeared to absorb the meaning of what he had just said. 'I've been far too hard on you,' he added abruptly.

Ellie was disconcerted to find herself being herded over to a sofa and urged to sit down. 'Dio... what on earth are you playing at?' she prompted weakly.

Dio came down beside her, his dark, devastatingly handsome features now stamped with taut discomfiture. 'You were *really* distressed after you saw that article. Even if you had announced your pregnancy to the entire maintenance staff in my building, I should have been more sympathetic towards your feelings.'

Ellie could agree with that, at least. However, she hadn't the slightest wish to shelter behind the excuse of emotional mood swings provoked by hormonal upheaval. 'Yes, but—'

'It just made me so bloody furious to see you being attacked in print!' Dio vented with sudden rawness as he folded a powerful arm round her and drew her close. 'And it was really chilling working out the sort of childhood you must have endured with two such selfish parents. That upset me too, and when I get upset, I blow a fuse. But when you dragged in Helena again, *fortunately* I began to see how wildly out of proportion this was all becoming.'

'I can't live with you not trusting me.'

'Of course I trust you…with one single exception,' Dio extended without hesitation. 'And I don't think we need to discuss that exception *again.*'

Ellie breathed in sharply. All she could taste was her own absolute defeat on the topic of Helena

Teriakos. She was shaken and upset. But how did she persist with her accusations? She didn't want to destroy their marriage before it even got going. Helena was already working hard at doing that. Hard *and* successfully, Ellie reflected painfully.

And how could she possibly fight the other woman without evidence? Was she about to sink to the humiliating level of begging Sally Parkes to repeat Helena's malicious verbal attack at their wedding? The sad truth was that no spiteful comment could possibly prove her own infinitely more serious allegations against the brunette.

'As for the newspaper foolish enough to print that rubbish, I shall sue,' Dio continued with chilling cool. 'My lawyers tell me I can hang them out to dry, and hang them I will.'

Involuntarily, Ellie shivered. 'Why bother?'

'When anyone attacks you, they're attacking me. Your reputation is at stake. I will defend it.'

'Well, don't feel you have to on my account,' Ellie muttered limply. 'Sticks and stones and all that—'

'They'll settle out of court and print a retraction. They will also make some worthy charity a most handsome donation.' Dio gazed searchingly at the pale delicacy of her set profile and curved her even closer. 'And before I'm finished with them, they'll also reveal their source.'

Ellie glanced at him in sudden hope, and then her eyes fell again. 'Journalists never do that.'

'You'd be surprised what they do behind closed doors when the pressure is great enough,' Dio asserted wryly. 'How are you feeling now?'

'That...that I want to be on my own,' Ellie confessed ruefully.

Dio tensed.

'I'm sorry. I just do.' Gently detaching herself from him, Ellie rose to her feet. 'I'll go for a walk.'

'I'll come with you.'

Ellie skimmed him a pained glance. 'No.'

She could see his frustration, *feel* it. And she loved him so much. If she didn't she wouldn't be in so much pain. But she needed time to wind down and come to terms with what had happened between them.

Ellie took the path down the beach house. Once she reached the warm soft sand on the beach, she kicked off her shoes and walked along through the surf whispering onto the shore. The sun shone blinding silvered reflections on the sea. It was hotter than it had been on her last visit. But she loved the heat. It seemed to drive out the chill inside her.

Here they were on the very first day of their honeymoon and Helena had already practically torn them apart, she reflected with a shiver. Dio had indeed been outraged by such lurid invasive publicity. And, whether she liked the role or not, Ellie now knew that she had become Dio's Achilles' heel. He *was* a very proud man, and she didn't want him to be any less proud. But they had had yet another violent and destructive argument and she had got precisely nowhere. How many more could they afford to have before Dio decided that their marriage had no future?

Ellie was far along the beach, sitting in the shade of a rocky outcrop, when she saw Dio striding towards her with lithe, long-limbed grace. He was carrying a picnic hamper.

'I did ask to be on my own,' Ellie reminded him gently.

'You've been on your own for three hours, *pethi mou*.' Black eyes held hers levelly. 'Now you need to eat.'

'Did the book Nathan made the mistake of giving you tell you that too?'

His lean, strong face clenched. 'So I want to be with you...is that a crime?'

Involuntarily, Ellie softened. 'No, I want to be with you too.'

'Only not enough to come back to the villa.'

Ellie considered that point and sighed. 'I have to admit that sometimes I really get a kick out of making you run after me.'

Dio looked startled. Then an appreciative laugh escaped him. 'I have never heard a woman admit that before.'

'Don't be slow, Dio. I'm only admitting it because we're married.'

His shimmering smile turned her heart over, and Ellie finally reached a decision. Dio might not recognise Helena's capacity for malice, but men were slow to recognise female cunning and Helena was clever. More importantly, Dio seemed quite happy with the wife he had. He wasn't behaving like a male who had given up the woman he loved. Or was he simply more pragmatic than she was prepared to acknowledge?

A frown drew Dio's level dark brows together. 'What are you thinking about?' he demanded.

Ellie gave him an innocent look. 'You,' she said with perfect truth.

A look somewhere between male pleasure and wariness formed on Dio's bronzed features, sunlight turning his eyes into reflective mirrors. 'Your expression seemed rather hostile—'

'I was just thinking that I want us to hang onto our marriage,' Ellie assured him piously.

The wary edge evaporated. Dio was now free to rejoice in the happy notion that he was at the heart of her every thought. And, yes, she noted with surprise, he liked that idea. She watched the slumbrous smile slowly curve his mouth. Only then did she acknowledge that he was indeed the very centre of her world. Perhaps it wasn't a good idea to let him know that.

'These days you need to work really hard to keep a marriage afloat,' she added.

'But we don't *have* any problems,' Dio stated with a definite aggressive edge.

Ellie busied herself rooting about in the incredibly elaborate picnic hamper and concealed the amused glint in her gaze. He was keen to deny the possibility that they did have a problem. And, having vented her spleen in setting Ellie up for that newspaper article, what, realistically, could Helena possibly do to hurt either her or their marriage in the future?

'My reaction to that squalid newspaper article was unreasonable,' Dio announced with real vigour.

Ellie glanced up. 'Was it?'

'There's scandal in my background too,' Dio assured her.

'Stop trying to make me feel better,' Ellie told him drily.

'My grandfather was temporarily disinherited for marrying my grandmother.'

'Polly and Lefki's sister?' Ellie queried in surprise. 'For goodness' sake, why?'

'She was an island girl. Her father was a...' Dio hesitated. 'Well, he kept goats,' he completed, rather grittily.

'He kept *goats*?' Ellie gasped incredulously.

'Don't say it...' Dio warned.

But for the next few seconds Ellie was quite incapable of saying anything. Recalling the way she had once compared Dio to a goat-herd, she started laughing so hard she flopped back on the sand. 'I'm sorry, Dio...I just love it!' she told him chokily.

'I knew I could rely on you to be tactful.' Leaning over her, Dio gazed down into her beautiful laughing face, black eyes flaring to smouldering gold.

Ellie trembled and raised her fingers to trace his hard jawline. 'How hungry are you?' she whispered unevenly.

And with a ragged groan of very male appreciation, Dio shifted over her. His mouth swooped down on hers in a hot, sensual invasion that spoke for itself.

Having carefully explored the sauna and gym complex in the basement of the enormous London townhouse, Ellie wandered on to study the fabulous indoor swimming pool, her eyes just getting wider and wider.

'I think you like this place,' Dio murmured.

'Hmm…it looks even better than it looked on the videotape the agent sent out to us,' Ellie confided.

'Then all we have to do is move in.'

Ellie spun round, her eyes lighting up. 'You love it too?'

'It seems to have everything, so we'll buy it.'

'It'll make such a marvellous family home!' Ellie threw both arms round Dio and then she frowned. Tilting back her head, she gave him an anxious, searching scrutiny. 'You're not buying it just to please me, are you?'

'Would I do that?'

'Yes,' she sighed. 'But this is where we're going to live. It's very important that you like it as much as I do. So give me your impressions.'

Dio shrugged. 'It'll make a terrific investment—'

Ellie groaned.

'The location *is* excellent—'

'Dio!' Ellie exclaimed in frustration.

He closed his arms round her, a slumbrous smile banishing his gravity. 'You rise to every bait there is, Mrs Alexiakis. I love the house…OK?'

'I'm sorry I made you go and see all the other ones, but I was scared we might be missing something,' Ellie admitted. 'Actually, the minute I saw this house on video I knew it was all my dreams come true, so I saved it to the last.'

Ellie climbed back into the limousine in a state of near bliss. They had been married for over a month now. They had spent three glorious weeks on Chindos, and Ellie had been so happy, she'd felt as if she was walking on air. She had been afraid that their return to London might take some of the magic away, yet, even though Dio was now frantically busy after taking so much time off, nothing had changed between them. They had shared so much more than a bed on the island: visits to Polly and Lefki's cosy little farmhouse, midnight swims, barbecues on the beach and so much laughter.

Now she was amazed that she had got herself in such a twist over Helena Teriakos. The brunette had taken her revenge with that newspaper article. Apart from the odd unavoidable social occasion, Ellie reckoned that the other woman was more or less out of their lives. Indeed, there was only one cloud in Ellie's world, and she knew it was a very selfish and unreasonable one.

She had a guy who would trail round a baby shop without complaint. She had a guy who acted as if the merest breathe of wind might blow her fragile little carcass away. She had a guy who *listened* when she talked, who was still sending her flowers after the wedding, and who phoned her in the mornings even if he was seeing her for lunch. A guy who was caring and supportive and absolutely incredible in bed. She was a really, really lucky woman. So wishing that Dio would fall madly in love with her as well was positively greedy.

Late that night, Dio strolled out of the bathroom in his penthouse apartment, towel loosely knotted about his lean hips, moisture still beading the curling dark tendrils of hair on his muscular chest. 'Ellie…there's something we need to talk about.'

Blissfully engaged in appreciating him, Ellie sat up in bed and smiled before she registered that his lean, dark features had a very serious cast. 'What's wrong?'

'There's nothing wrong,' Dio asserted wryly. 'I'm flying over to Paris to see Helena tomorrow.'

Ellie blinked in sheer shock.

'Naturally I'm hoping that this won't cause trouble between us,' Dio continued levelly. 'Since her father died I have been in charge of all Helena's business interests.'

At that second revelation, an appalled look froze Ellie's fine features. 'Why didn't you tell me that before?' she demanded.

'To be blunt,' Dio murmured steadily, black eyes challenging her now, 'I really don't think that a responsibility I accepted long before I met you is any real concern of yours.'

Ellie turned pale. That wasn't just blunt, that was brutal.

Dio released his breath in an impatient hiss. 'I want you to be rational about the fact that I meet up with Helena on a regular basis.'

'Rational…' Her husband met up with her most bitter enemy on a regular basis. That news was the equivalent of being slugged with a sandbag.

Dio came down on her side of the bed and reached for her hand.

Ellie snatched it back.

'Can't you even try to behave like a grown-up?' Dio censured with stark impatience as he sprang upright again. 'I accept that you felt insecure when we *first* got married—'

Ellie parted bloodless lips. 'Mr Sensitive—'

'But now you've had time to settle down—'

'You think so?' Ellie breathed shakily.

'I think you've got no choice,' Dio delivered with sudden harshness, surveying her with cool dark eyes.

'There's always a choice, Dio.'

'Not on this issue,' Dio contradicted. 'I will continue to oversee Helena's business holdings for as long as she wishes me to do so. Our meetings will also continue. She's a part of my life and you have to accept that.'

'That's not something I can accept.' Ellie lifted her head high, colour burning in her cheeks. Suddenly she was furious with herself. 'What an idiot I've been!' she exclaimed. 'All my life I've stood up for myself, but I wanted our marriage to work and I didn't want to tear us apart.'

'What are you trying to say?'

'You refused to accept that Helena threatened me and tried to bribe me into having an abortion.'

Dio raked long brown fingers through his tousled damp black hair and groaned out loud. 'Oh, *please*, not that nonsense again!'

'You don't believe me. OK. Right. That's fine,' Ellie said jerkily, punching the pillows and lying down. 'Nice to know where your loyalty lies, Dio. Nice to know that you married me thinking I was a liar—'

'But kind of cute with it,' Dio incised gently.

'Don't try to make a joke out of something this important!' Ellie condemned. 'If you go to Paris tomorrow, I'm leaving you!'

Dio stilled. 'No way would you leave me—'

'Yes, I would! You trust her more than you trust me. So you make your choice,' Ellie told him bitterly. 'You get her out of your life, where she can't hurt us any more, or I'm moving out! If you can't give me one hundred per cent loyalty, I don't want you any more!'

'No problem,' Dio said softly.

Ellie listened to him walking out of the room, and then she leapt out of bed and hauled the door open. 'I *mean* it, Dio!'

Shorn of his towel and magnificently nude, Dio

swung round and gazed back at her with outraged dark eyes. 'You do as you like, but I'm going to Paris and I won't be hurrying back.'

All the pain inside Ellie mushroomed. 'Dio...I'm *not* lying. Listen to me—'

Dio stabbed a powerful hand in the air. 'No, *you* listen to me! You don't own me. You don't tell me what I can do, where I can go or who I can be with. Is that understood?'

'That—'

'And when you've got this jealousy jag under control, call me. But don't leave it too long. After all, Helena is a lot of things you're not,' Dio murmured in derisive retaliation.

The angry colour drained from Ellie's complexion.

Dio said something vicious in Greek and strode back towards her.

Ellie slammed the bedroom door in his face and depressed the lock.

'Ellie!' Dio thundered. 'Open that door!'

Tears running down her face, Ellie crawled into bed again and curled up in a tight ball. 'A lot of things you're not.' Well, trust Dio to state the obvious. Only it wasn't a matter of that, was it? In temper, he had revealed his true feelings, and the horribly wounding comparisons he obviously continued to make. Ellie shivered, acknowledging that the furious row that had blown up had drawn more blood than she had bargained on. Her *own*.

Helena was rich, educated, classy, cool, controlled, clever. Her background was identical to his own. Of course, Dio admired and respected her. Unlike Ellie, Helena would have been a bride he could have been really proud of possessing.

'The English rely on love… It's more important to pick a life partner with intelligence,' he had told her that very first night on the beach. But what had intelligence had to do with their shotgun wedding? Ellie muffled sobs in a pillow. For the past few weeks Dio had been *very* good at pretending to be happy. All those years of smoothie womanising, she supposed wretchedly. In his heart, Dio knew she was a very poor but pregnant second best. And Ellie knew that *she* couldn't live with him knowing that…

CHAPTER TEN

SALLY PARKES' anxious face lit up with a hugely relieved smile the instant she saw Ellie walking across the park towards her.

'Thank goodness you didn't stand me up!' she gasped as she flew off the bench.

Ellie dug her hands into the pockets of her jacket. 'I really didn't want to meet up with you like this, Sally. I only phoned you because I need you to pass on a message to Dio. I appreciate now that that was wrong of me—'

'No! No way was it wrong!'

'It was,' Ellie sighed. 'I didn't want to write to Dio because I didn't know what to say...and I didn't want to speak to him personally. But I never should've involved you—'

Sally groaned. 'Ellie...Dio is frantic!'

Ellie frowned. 'Didn't you pass on my message?'

Sally gave her a wide-eyed look of wonder. 'Like telling Dio you were safe and happy and planning on a divorce was going to make him *less* frantic?'

Ellie flushed. 'It's for the best. Did you remember to tell him that I'll let him see the baby as much as he likes?'

'It wasn't quite the consolation you seemed to think it would be,' Sally responded. 'I mean the baby's not due for another six months.'

'Well, I can't help that,' Ellie muttered flatly. 'Is he still in Paris?'

'No, according to Nathan he spent that week looking for you. Then he went off on the most dreadful drinking binge. Nathan dragged him home to sleep it off in our spare room—'

Ellie stopped dead. 'The most dreadful...*what*? Say that again?'

'OK. Sequence of events: Dio wakes up and finds your note...right?'

'I don't know. I'd gone by then. I thought he would have gone on to Paris.'

That very same night Ellie had thrown a few things in a bag and had crept out of the apartment, determined to avoid another harrowing confrontation with Dio. She had lost enough face in that earlier scene. All she'd had left was her pride. And she would only keep her pride by staying at a safe distance from Dio until she'd got her emotions under better control.

'Well, if you'll excuse me for saying so, most husbands wouldn't get dumped and just go on like it was an ordinary day,' Sally said rather drily. 'Even stubborn, macho ones like Dio have *some* feelings.'

'Look, you're on his side because you don't understand and you know him better than you know me—'

'No, to be honest, I've just been totally gobsmacked by the way Dio's been carrying on,' Sally shared helplessly. 'I never, ever thought Dio would be sleeping off a hangover in our spare room.'

'So he spent the first week looking for me...' Ellie was hopelessly hungry for every tiny detail she could glean.

'How do you think we found out you'd gone? He phoned Nathan. He was in a real rage at that point. You were lucky to stay lost,' Sally confided.

'I don't understand him drinking...'

'He just went to pieces the second week. He sat in that apartment just drinking himself into a stupor, and Nathan was worried sick about him. Dio doesn't *do* things like that. You've really gutted him, Ellie...and I think that if you'd decided you wanted out, you could have been a lot more considerate about the way you did it.' Sally gave her a challenging glance.

Ellie tilted her chin, although her colour had risen. 'I told him I was leaving.'

'He didn't think you *meant* it!'

'It just wasn't working for me.'

Sally slowly shook her head with a bemused frown. 'The day of your wedding, I honestly thought you were crazy about him, and when we had lunch the week after you got back from Chindos it seemed even more pronounced. It was "Dio *this*…Dio *that*…"'

'I am crazy about him,' Ellie mumbled ruefully.

Sally fell still. 'Then why the heck are you doing this to him?' she demanded.

'I suppose you've told her absolutely everything, Sally,' Dio's dark growl intervened with sardonic grittiness. 'The big search, the unmanly despair, the buckets of booze and self-pity…'

Both women whipped around. Sally hot-cheeked, Ellie pale as death.

But Dio had eyes only for his estranged wife. As Sally backed away with a guilty grimace, his dark, deep-set gaze welded to Ellie's pinched and shaken face and stayed there. 'I've really messed up, haven't I?'

'Dio…can I give you just a little hint that that is not the right attitude to take?' Sally prompted with a wince.

'No…you don't know what's going on here and you're not going to,' Dio informed the redhead with bleak satisfaction. 'Isn't it fortunate that when I'm drunk I talk in Greek? No, Sally. What this is all about will be one mystery you never manage to solve.'

'Helena…' The redhead murmured with measured female superiority before she drifted off.

Dio flinched, and his bronzed skin lost colour.

'Considering that Sally set me up for you, you weren't very polite,' Ellie said unevenly. 'I'd never have come to meet her if I'd known you were planning to show up.'

'Sally tortured me with questions when I was at my lowest ebb. And even the worst sinners get their moment to speak on judgement day,' Dio breathed with an attempted lightness that was laced with strain.

Ellie stared back at him, her heart thumping like a hammer behind her ribs, her eyes full of pain.

'Don't look at me like that…it makes it so much worse,' Dio groaned.

Instantly Ellie looked away. Yes, of course he

would see how she felt. He always had been able to see inside her. Crushed by the awareness that even her love was obvious to him, she made no demur when he curved a surprisingly tentative arm round her and walked her away. The limousine was collecting a parking ticket beyond the park gates. Dio felt guilty. Obviously he felt guilty. He knew how much he had hurt her. And what was to be gained in trying to avoid a meeting that he was determined to force on her?

In the silence, Ellie stole a glance at him as the opulent car purred through the slow-moving traffic. In two and a half weeks he had contrived to lose quite a bit of weight, she noted. And now it was as if a divide the width of an immeasurable abyss separated them. She had never dreamt that Dio could look as downright sombre as he did now. The end of a marriage. Well, he wasn't so superficial that he was about to celebrate, particularly when she would be giving birth to their child in a few months' time.

'It's OK,' she said flatly.

'Nothing's OK,' Dio countered harshly. 'Where have you been staying?'

'A B&B out in the suburbs. I didn't feel like the

hassle of looking for somewhere more permanent yet,' she admitted stiltedly.

'Didn't it occur to you that I'd be going out of my mind with worry?' he demanded with sudden force.

'Why should it have?' Ellie sighed. 'I've been looking after myself for a heck of a long time. I'm not the helpless type.'

The silence seemed to thunder.

'No,' Dio conceded gruffly. 'But you can make *me* feel helpless.'

Her brow furrowed. 'Oh, you mean you looking for me and not being able to find me?' she gathered. 'There was no need for that. I wasn't planning to vanish for ever, or anything stupid like that. I made that clear in my note—'

'*Ne*…yes: "Dio, I'm sorry, but I had to empty your wallet to get some cash."' Dio quoted the opening line of her note flatly. '"Marrying you was a mistake. I'll be in touch. Don't look for me…but then I don't suppose you will, will you?"'

'I don't see why you have to quote the whole thing,' Ellie protested, feeling even more foolish and exposed by that verbatim delivery. 'I was upset and I didn't have much time. You're lucky you *got* a note!'

Instead of exploding at that rather unjust stab, Dio froze in his distant corner of the back seat. 'I guess you're right about that.'

Ellie sent him a slightly bewildered glance, registering the raw tension etched into his bold, dark profile. 'I honestly didn't think you might get worried until later—'

'Much later. It took you eleven days to phone Sally,' Dio reminded her tautly.

'I had some stuff to work out.'

Like how to live without him, how to exist with a ceaseless craving that got more agonising with every passing hour, how to close out the flawed memory of good times that could only have been utterly superficial on his terms. Great sex, she had assumed on their honeymoon, but dared she assume even that now? For her, making love with Dio had been earth-shattering sensational perfection. But how did she *really* know what it had been like for him? He had been flatteringly insatiable, but maybe he was just rampantly oversexed, she reflected grimly.

'So what have you been doing with yourself?'

'I've been making plans.' Actually, she had done nothing but walk around all day, sit in the public library when she got tired, eat for the baby's sake and use up boxes of tissues at night. However, it would have taken torture to force an admission like that from her.

She had climbed out of the limo before she realised that they had not arrived at Dio's apartment building. Her bewildered gaze absorbed the tall, imposing Georgian townhouse they had viewed the same day they'd parted. 'What on earth are we doing *here*?'

'I went ahead and bought it.'

'You did say it would be a good investment,' Ellie recalled as she opened the front door.

'I was joking.'

Had he been? Ellie had spent two and a half wretched weeks picking apart everything Dio had ever said or done, seeking evidence with which to bolster up her resistance level. Waste of time, she now conceded gloomily. One look at him, even in this strange, muted mode he appeared to be in, and she was back where she had been that first night on Chindos. Mesmerised. Poised there in his exquisitely tailored charcoal-grey suit, he was so gorgeous he still took her breath away.

'What did you do with the rest of my things?' Ellie asked to fill the simmering silence.

Dio frowned. 'They're here.'

'Where?'

'In the main bedroom.'

'Oh, right. You didn't tell the staff that I wasn't coming back.' Ellie started up the grand staircase.

'Where are you going?'

Ellie barely glanced over her shoulder. 'I might as well get my stuff packed up while I'm here,' she said briskly. 'It'll save me another trip.'

'Ellie…' Dio began heavily. 'I know I've acted like a total four-letter word—'

'Dio, I don't need to hear that sort of stuff.' Ellie marched on up the staircase at an even faster rate of knots. 'This is nobody's fault. We only got married because I was pregnant, which was just plain stupid…OK? It's no big deal, is it?'

'No big deal?' Dio repeated thickly.

Ellie could not resist the urge to turn and peer down at him from the landing, but he had swung away. 'Look, all I'm trying to say is I don't want to talk about it. There's no need.'

Dio appeared in the dressing room doorway while Ellie was frantically trailing clothes off hangers. Her hands were all thumbs. What on earth had possessed her? In another minute she would either crumple into humiliating hysterical tears or she would seize him by the throat and ask him how he could possibly prefer Arctic Woman to her.

'Helena *was* behind that disgusting tabloid attack on you...'

Ellie stilled, and then suddenly jerked round, eyes very wide.

Dio stared back at her with tormented dark eyes shimmering with strain, his hands clenched into powerful fists by his side. His vibrant skin had a greyish cast.

'I suppose she came off that pedestal you had her on with a real shocking crash...' Ellie's heart felt as if it was cracking right down the middle, and she felt that if she didn't keep on talking she might be at serious risk of starting to sob. Everything she had never wanted to see was etched in Dio's face. His appalled reaction to Helena's true nature.

'I didn't have her on a—'

'I'm sorry, Dio. But you know a woman would have spotted her for what she was a mile off! But then...' Ellie altered direction hurriedly, not wishing to come across as spiteful 'Isn't it comforting to know that she was that determined to get you back?'

'Only because...only because of who I am and what I have.'

'Yeah, well,' Ellie managed with a sickly smile. 'Be honest. You valued those same things in her. All that background and breeding and money.'

Dio just closed his eyes and bowed his proud head. 'I don't expect you to forgive me for refusing to believe you.'

'Good. I wasn't going to make the offer.' Ellie turned back to the built-in units which blurred in front of her eyes. 'I understand that you thought that she was above all that kind of thing, and that you're feeling pretty bad now you know the truth… how *do* you, by the way?' she prompted with sudden curiosity.

'A journalist sang like a canary bird. Helena had had you investigated.'

'I could have told you that.'

'She set up a meeting with a reporter and handed over the file. She gave it on the understanding that the article would vilify and humiliate you.' Dio's dark, deep drawl roughened tellingly. 'She was too arrogant to even *try* to cover her tracks.'

'Maybe she thought it would be more of a risk to trust somebody else with that file.' Tears were inching down Ellie's cheeks, but she kept on hauling garments blindly off hangers as she struggled to get a grip on herself.

'Did you see the interview I gave about you?'

Ellie's wet eyes widened with bemusement. 'No…'

'I hoped it would bring you out of hiding. I knew you had promised to meet Sally today, but she warned me that she'd had to fight to get you to agree,' Dio disclosed tautly. 'And when you would only set a date a whole week in advance…frankly, I thought there was little hope that you would actually turn up.'

'I wouldn't have done that to Sally. She's a nice person.'

'When I faced Helena with what she had done, she kept on lying very convincingly for a long time. Then I mentioned the malice Sally had heard her spitting at you on our wedding day—'

'Isn't it wonderful the way you believed everyone *but* me? That journalist? Sally?' Ellie condemned with tremulous but very fierce bitterness.

'I honestly could never have imagined Helena capable of such behaviour,' Dio framed grittily. 'That is…until two weeks ago, when I confronted her and she finally lost her temper because she realised that she had lost.'

'She didn't *lose*, Dio. She won all the way,' Ellie contradicted flatly, her tears drying on her cheeks now. 'We didn't have much to start out with…and by the time she'd finished we had nothing. But don't you kid yourself that she was the one *most* at fault!'

'I know where the blame lies. I know I let you down and made you very unhappy. You hate me, don't you?'

'Some of the time…like right now, *yes*!' Ellie suddenly snapped as she rounded on him, her green eyes emerald with anger. 'She really scared me that day with her threats. She'd have done anything to persuade me into getting rid of our baby! She sneered at my mother, she insulted me every way possible and you wouldn't even *listen*.'

Dio moved forward. 'Ellie…I—'

'Shut up!' Ellie interrupted furiously. 'I was a total idiot to marry you in the first place! I was very upset that day—'

'You had every right to be. All I know is that I have never been closer to violence than I was when confronting Helena two weeks ago,' Dio revealed with raw force. 'The manner in which she spoke of you almost drove me to assault!'

'Really?' Ellie was quite happy to rein back temper long enough to relish that enervating detail.

'So does that mean that there's *not* going to be a reconciliation?'

Dio stared back at her blankly.

'You're not planning to marry her after me, then?' Ellie rephrased.

'Are you unhinged? *Marry her?*' Dio exclaimed incredulously. 'She's a cold, vicious bitch!'

'Well, it took you a lifetime, but in the end you got there. Congratulations,' Ellie said very drily. 'Could you get me a case?'

'A case?'

Ellie was possessed by the need to keep busy. Dio was getting to her and she had been determined that he was not going to get to her. That five-letter word labelling Helena as beyond the pale, for all her background, breeding and brilliance, had blown a small hole in Ellie's defences. She moved forward and then almost fell over the mound of clothing heaped round her. She looked down in astonishment at what appeared to be a whole heap of Dio's suits.

Sidestepping them, she attempted to brush past Dio. He closed his hand over hers. 'You've got to hear me out!' he grated rawly.

'You didn't hear *me* out, did you? No, when I was trying to state my case either I was insane with jealousy or off my trolley with being pregnant! And shall I tell you something, Dio? Right now, I'm near *my* personal edge!' Ellie vented with ringing honesty. 'Let…go…of…me!'

Dio released her with a jerk. Dark colour scored his stunning cheekbones but it was the savage pain in the depths of his dark eyes that shook her. 'I am more sorry that I have hurt you than you will ever believe,' he breathed raggedly.

Pale and trembling from that charged exchange, Ellie went off in search of a suitcase. It was mad, it was *crazy* to keep on trying to pack in the midst of such emotional turmoil, but she couldn't bear to see Dio in so much pain; she really couldn't! All over the head of that evil witch, who had almost sucked him in like a boa constrictor! Ellie shuddered as she banged through the closets she recalled touring two and a half weeks earlier. Locating the designated luggage storage, she grabbed up a case.

'Let me take that…' Dio took it from her again.

'You know…you don't feel it now, but sooner or later, you'll realise what a lucky escape you've had,' she muttered half under her breath, and hurried back to the master bedroom suite that they would now never share.

'Ellie…please sit down so that we can talk,' Dio urged, sounding almost pathetically humble. 'I need to tell you about Helena.'

Ellie was so appalled by that confession she sank down on the side of the bed before her legs gave out beneath her. If he needed a shoulder, why did it have to be hers? Then she understood. He wanted to make a complete confession. Nothing less would satisfy his over-active conscience. So he was about to drag out personal admissions that would very probably rip her heart out and depress her for the next thirty years.

Dio regarded her warily and very slowly set down the case. He cleared his throat. 'I—'

'Will you keep it short?' Ellie begged without pride.

Dio got even tenser. He looked so absolutely miserable her heart went out to him. She had to face it now. He had really loved Helena. He might now be repulsed, but he *had* loved her.

'My father first told me that Helena would make me a wonderful wife when I was five.'

'*Five*…five years old?' Ellie yelped. 'What age was she?'

'Eight.'

'Five…dear heaven, that's like brainwashing!' Ellie said in disgust.

'My grandparents died in a car accident when my father was still very young. He was brought up by his father's family. You must understand that my father was made to feel very much ashamed of his mother's more humble ancestry.'

'So he was raised to be a real snob?'

Dio nodded.

'And he wanted to be sure you didn't let the side down?'

Dio nodded again.

'So you were indoctrinated from a very early age to believe that Helena was your future.'

'A future I kept putting off.' Dio breathed in deep. 'I could never admit even to myself that I didn't like Helena—'

'You didn't…*like* Helena?' Ellie interrupted in astonishment.

'Did you find her a warm, inviting personality when you first came in contact with her on Chindos?'

'*No*, but—'

Dio's jawline hardened. 'I could never fault her behaviour. Her every accomplishment was continually paraded before me, and she is very accomplished. It was instilled in me that I had to marry her.'

'So you decided you'd marry her and have a mistress to supply the warmth she so conspicuously lacks.'

Recognising her scorn, Dio dealt her a wry look of reproach. 'Such marriages are not uncommon in my world. Until I met you, I didn't realise what I might be missing.'

Ellie sighed. 'I can't believe that.'

'OK…so there have been a few women in my past,' Dio conceded, in distinctly charged understatement. 'But not one of them got to me the way you did. We had that one magical night and then I blew it. But I couldn't stay away from you—'

'So you married me and blew it again,' Ellie slotted in painfully.

Dio crossed the carpet and hunkered down to look up into her wan face. He tried to reach for her hands. She put them behind her back.

Dio's mouth quirked. 'The night you told me that you might be pregnant, I realised that I was in love with you—head over heels in love.'

'You would tell me *anything* to keep a hold on our baby, wouldn't you?' Ellie mumbled with a sob in her voice.

Dio's beautiful dark eyes shimmered. He un-peeled her hands from behind her back and held them fast in his. 'My biggest mistake was not telling you how I felt that night in my apartment,' he told her rawly. 'I knew then that I would *never* marry Helena, and that's when the guilt kicked in. Then she phoned after we had made love and I felt even worse!'

A little shard of hope pierced Ellie's emotional turmoil. Now she was locked onto his every facial expression, his every word. She remembered the way he had reacted after that phone call that had interrupted them. 'You should have explained about her then!'

Dio released his breath in a rueful hiss. 'I didn't want to upset you. I also didn't feel right talking to you about her at that stage,' he admitted. 'First I needed to see her and tell her that I had fallen in love.'

'Is that what you told her?'

Dio gave her a questioning look. 'What else would I have told her? I knew she wouldn't be too impressed by the announcement, but it was the truth. When you came out of Nathan's surgery, I really was pleased about the baby, but I'm afraid my guilt over Helena ruined what should've been a very special occasion.'

'I can understand how you must've felt.'

Dio grimaced. 'No, you can't. I was very angry with myself for letting that understanding with Helena drift on for so long. I believed that I was letting her down very badly,' he confessed. 'But if I felt bad then, it was nothing to how I felt when I actually faced Helena in Paris.'

Ellie frowned, her hands tightening their hold on his. 'What did she do to you?'

'She played me like a violin,' Dio grated with a perceptible rise of blood to his bronzed complexion as he recalled that meeting. 'She said that she would be a laughing stock, and that no man would ever marry her if I didn't. But she kept on reiterating that of course she understood and forgave me...I was there for *hours*!' He gave a feeling shudder of recollection. 'I felt like a complete bastard. I honestly thought that I had ruined her life.'

'She's a terrific actress...or maybe...maybe she really does love you, Dio,' Ellie suggested unhappily.

Dio gave her an aghast look. 'You've got to be joking!'

'I love you...why shouldn't she? She's known you a lot longer—'

'Ellie...' Dio vaulted upright and carried her with

him, his dark eyes ablaze with intense pleasure and relief at that simple confession. 'Ellie, darling, darling, gorgeous Ellie…' he breathed raggedly. 'If I was a poor man, Helena wouldn't give me the time of day. She's obsessed with marrying a wealthy man worthy of her illustrious family tree. She simply could not credit that I could be *wet* enough to start talking about love…she said I could have you if I wanted you—'

'As a mistress—'

'And I said I loved you too much for that.' Dio brushed her hair from her brow with gentle fingers, so much tenderness in his warm dark eyes that Ellie finally believed that he loved her. 'But when I confronted her two weeks ago, she was much more honest. She assured me that if a better matrimonial prospect had come along, she'd have been married years ago!'

'I'm glad she was angry rather than hurt,' Ellie admitted.

'Even after all she's done to you?' Dio demanded with naked incredulity.

Ellie stretched up to loosen his tie in a very proprietorial way. 'I can be very generous when I've won,' she shared rather smugly.

Dio caught her up in his arms and crushed her

mouth with hungry intensity beneath his. As he buried his face in her hair, she quivered, feeling as weak as a kitten.

'I never dreamt that hearing a woman telling me that she loved me could mean so much,' he confided with roughened sincerity.

'And to think that if you had told me rather than Helena,' Ellie could not resist remarking, 'that you *loved* me, I'd never have left you.'

'Don't you ever leave me again,' Dio warned fiercely.

'I wouldn't dream of it...' She gave him a teasing glance, rejoicing in this new intimacy of mutual trust which allowed her to do and say what she liked. 'Not if it means you're likely to drown in buckets of booze and self-pity...'

Dio brought her down on the bed and pinned her there, black eyes alight with immense appreciation. 'You are a minx.'

'I've got your number now...you'd better watch out...'

'I adore you,' he husked feelingly. 'But you're not going to boss me around.'

Ellie slid loving fingers into his luxuriant black hair and whispered, 'Kiss me...'

And he did.

Then he lifted his head with a glint of mocking comprehension in his keen gaze. 'Pregnant, barefoot and in the bedroom, *agapi mou*,' he told her slumbrously.

'You're misquoting.'

A slashing smile curved Dio's mouth. 'It was a statement of intent.'

'Well, if we're negotiating, what about all that "You don't tell me what I can do, where I can go or who I can be with" stuff?' Ellie enquired playfully.

'I just knew you would remember every word of that.'

'Because I reserve the *right* to.'

'You could have been a real *agent provocateur* in the maintenance department.' His brilliant dark eyes roamed over her and glittered with desire and boundless satisfaction. 'It's far safer keeping you in my bed.'

'I've got to admit the family cave's pretty comfortable,' Ellie sighed happily, sparing her impressive surroundings a look of approval.

And, with a husky laugh of appreciation, Dio kissed her breathless and proceeded to demonstrate the fringe benefits of sharing that family cave.

* * *

Ellie tucked her infant son, Spiros, back into his exquisite cradle. At four months old, Spiros was just adorable. He had hair the colour of silver-gilt and dark, dark eyes—an arresting combination of his parental genes. When he was sound asleep, he looked like a little angel.

The past twenty-four hours had been hectic, Ellie acknowledged. Dio had thrown a huge party in London to celebrate their first wedding anniversary. Then they had flown out to the island and spent the day entertaining Dio's relatives, who had now all either gone to bed or travelled home again.

A whole year. Ellie could still hardly credit that she had been married to Dio for that long. And the magic had not only lasted but got stronger, she reflected, with glowing eyes and the slow, steady smile of a contented woman.

Working conditions in the maintenance department of Alexiakis International were now as good as they could get. Dio had never quite recovered from the sight of Ellie plugging in that floor-polisher and then fainting dead away. Ellie had had no trouble convincing him that the cleaning staff deserved more generous remuneration for their rarely appreciated efforts.

Ellie returned to their bedroom to slide into a

very sexy confection of gold satin, a special order fashioned along the lines of a flamenco dress. Setting off to the beach house, after having instructed a maid to deliver her surprise note to Dio, Ellie took with her the glossy magazine that gushingly described Helena Teriakos' wedding the previous week. She hadn't had a chance to finish reading the article yet.

The bridegroom was a blue-blooded aristocrat, with a title a yard long. Helena looked positively triumphant. However, it was rumoured that the non-attendance of the groom's powerful family signified their outrage at his choice of bride. On their terms it seemed that Helena was just *not* acceptable. Her family tree only went back a couple of generations, while theirs went back several centuries. But, studying the photo of the bridal couple, Ellie reckoned it would be a successful marriage. Helena's husband looked like Arctic Man, his cold blue eyes, tight mouth and rigid carriage.

Slinging the magazine aside with a smile, Ellie lit all the candles and switched off the lights. Then she began to dance to the music she had put on to accompany her display. This was her private anniversary present to Dio. She loved to surprise him. And when she caught the door opening out of the corner of her eye, she had to work really hard not to be drawn into looking directly at him.

When the music rose to a savage crescendo and ended, then she looked, and just burned beneath the sheer, glittering hunger and appreciation in Dio's stunning eyes.

'You are just *so* easily impressed!' she teased.

Dio hauled her into his arms just like a caveman. She was shivering with excitement. Sensual anticipation ran like fire through her veins, leaving her weak as he slowly crushed her into the hard, muscular heat of his big powerful body. 'So we're back where we started out—'

'Plus Spiros.'

'I never forget our son for a single moment... or the very beautiful, very sexy and wonderful woman who gave him to me,' Dio intoned with impressive intensity. 'I think I love you even more now than I did a year ago.'

Ellie closed her arms round him tightly. 'You make me so happy.'

'That's what I'm here for...' Somewhat distracted by his need to seal his mouth hotly to hers while at the same time backing towards the bedroom, Dio finally contrived the feat and got them both as far as the bed. 'And to give you *this*...before you dare to suggest that I rushed down here in the most un-cool manner imaginable just because I could not wait to go to bed with you!'

Ellie gazed down at the exquisite diamond eternity ring he was now sliding onto her finger and she just melted back into him. 'Oh, Dio…it's *gorgeous.*'

'It's engraved with the date we first met.'

'Gosh, you're getting so romantic!' Ellie sighed.

Dio looked exceedingly smug. 'You may have set up the candles and the note, but I brought the champagne and had a rose put on the pillow.'

Ellie's eyes widened and her face fell. 'You mean my note wasn't a surprise?'

Dio winced, registering the error of one-upmanship.

A slow, misty smile curved Ellie's generous mouth and she pushed Dio gently back against the pillows. 'I just love you to death when you drop yourself in a big tactless hole,' she told him helplessly.

'I don't quite follow that.' Dio surveyed her with adoring eyes that had a definite hint of bemused relief.

Ellie arranged herself sinuously round him, knowing he didn't understand. But that anxious look he had worn when he had feared that he had hurt her feelings just turned her heart inside out. 'Great minds think alike,' she whispered soothingly.

'You are just amazing...' Dio curved her so close she could hardly breathe.

But then, at the moment, breathing was not half as important as the urgent need to seal their love in the most intimate way of all. Ellie meant to tell him just how amazing he was as well. But the electrifying combination of passion and joyous happiness now unleashed ensured that she didn't tell him until the following morning.

* * * * *